T://Error404
By
Allisha McAdoo

About the author

I started writing when I was a little girl and found out at an early age that I enjoyed horror. Over the years I continued to write horror and finding ways to hone my craft. I enjoy creating characters only to drag them to hell and back. I enjoy scaring people and grossing them out to the point where like a train wreck they can't stop reading. I recently started publishing things on Amazon. I recently had someone ask me why I chose to write about humans as monsters. To be honest, I can write about ghosts or vampires or anything like that, but to me people will always be the monsters. Growing up, ghosts and shadows kept me company as the people hurt me. Each story I have written is my way of coping with things, it's my therapy. Over the years as I got older, my monsters have become my muse. I write in an extreme fashion because it comes easy to me. My stories are not for the faint of heart, or the meek. My stories can be terrifying. When people in my waking life get to know me they are surprised that someone who looks like myself can write about such darkness. All

I can say to that, is I am not like most people. Lol.

If you like this one be sure to check me out, because there are going to be more published.

My group
https://www.facebook.com/groups/171880 2991696554/

My facebook author page
https://www.facebook.com/allishamcadoo author/

My amazon page (Where you can find my other ebooks on kindle and goodreads)
https://www.amazon.com/s/ref=nb_sb_s s_i_4_6?url=search-alias%3Daps&field-keywords=allisha+mcadoo&sprefix=allish %2Caps%2C205&crid=1XQBXSJGNHP0

My author central page
amazon.com/author/allishamcadoo

My other paperbacks are:
Dark Desires (a collaboration with Thomas J Kline)
Playthings with the devil (a short story collection)
Mr. Nice Guy (My first novel)
Your dirty secret (two of Mr. Rumple stories.)
Night Terrors (A short story collaboration with J.M Swiger)
Forever Together (3rd novel)
Yours for a price (Mr. Rumple origin story)
Twisted Sideways (Short story collection that ties every story together)

Coming soon

Fatal tales (A collaboration with Howard Carlyle)
Flesh puppets (a dark version of Goldilocks & the 3 bears)

Author's note

Warning This story contains graphic materials that some may not find suitable. This story came to me over the years and in a strange way is my way of exercising my demons. All this turmoil played a major part of my brain plunging me into darkness for a while. Welcome to my revenge, my carefully sought out hell for my characters. I started writing this story in 2020 because it is a chapter I want to close indefinitely. Keep in mind I do not tolerate any of the behavior depicted in my characters. I merely wrote this story to move through some parts of my past. This is my way of telling my demons to fuck off as I continue to move forward in my life. If this story is too much for you, you don't have to read it. You can go to any library and check out Dr. Seuss. I try to put supernatural elements into all my horror stories, and if that's something you don't like then this story is not for you. I like to intermingle different genres together. It may not be a plausible story, but it's a story I am proud of. I write for me, because it's the only way to keep moving forward with my life without getting stuck in my past's quicksand.

As I have said before people are monsters and therefore I will write them as such. This story is designed to push every emotional button with you. It's designed to keep you awake at night and to keep you looking over your shoulder. I hope you enjoy it.

PART 1

"Deep into that darkness peering, long I stood there, wondering, fearing, doubting, dreaming dreams no mortal ever dared to dream before." Edgar Allen Poe

Prologue

"This will be the last one!" I said, putting a huge stack of papers on my partner's desk. "What is all that?" She asked peering over her reading glasses that no one else knew she wore. "This is a print out of the conversation this stupid prick and I engaged in. He was only talking to me because he thinks I am an 8 year old girl. Meet Jason DeVont, he is a pedophile. Not just that, but this one is way personal. He was my first love, and when we do apprehend him, he is going to Mitch. "

"Woah, I have never heard you say that. This guy must really boil your blood." My partner said quietly as she began to read over the conversation. "Don't worry. You can count on me. We will get this guy. I'll miss working with you, but the pay will be nice. You had always said the last one would pay the most. " She said as she flipped a page. "T://error404? What a stupid name for the internet." She snorted as she began to read. I nodded,

"That's right, this one will pay for your retirement. This one will also complete Mitch's contract. He chose it because it spells out terror and the 404 is his favorite number. Something about a computer term I believe. " I realized I was holding my breath and let it out with a whoosh. "This is going to be epic! I will get to finding him as quickly as possible." She said carefully removing her glasses. I nodded thinking about everything, my last one.

"Hey Lollie, do you want to hear the story from the beginning?" I asked as I started to make coffee at my desk. " Definitely, this one you said is personal, so spill the entire story while I search for his last whereabouts." Lollie smiled and started to start up her laptop.

Suddenly, my chest felt tight and I couldn't breathe. The beginning. I would have to dwell into my relationship with Jason. I did my best to clear my throat. "It all started 20 years ago, and yes I know that is a very long time to hunt him down. Out of all of the bastards on my list to punish, this one I saved for last." I paused drinking a drink from my freshly brewed coffee.

Chapter 1

Year 2000 High School

In the year of 2000 I was just starting highschool. I had finally turned 14 three days before school started. I was nervous and shy because I had finally gotten my braces off. My hair was super poofy after falling asleep with wet braids. I looked like a scared gazelle with straight teeth and poofy hair. The outfit I had originally picked out to wear got ruined from my brother throwing up on it. I ended up wearing the only thing I had clean which was a too tight pair of shorts and a wild plaid shirt that hung off my shoulders.

The shirt was entirely ugly and the shorts made it hard to breathe, let alone move.

All I could do was clutch my books to my chest and try to blend in with the sea of bodies. My anxiety levels were completely off the charts, yet somehow I managed to make it to most of my classes without getting lost or throwing up. By the first week, I had gotten everything down pretty well to the point where no one even noticed me. I ended up taking an acting class by mistake instead of the class I really wanted. I spent a week trying to get out of it, however, I stayed enrolled in the acting class where I met Jason DeVont. Jason was the same height and weight as myself but had jet black hair with eyes to match. His voice sounded like he was being strangled but strangely that didn't bother me. It was raspy yet I found myself enjoying hearing his voice.

Jason was 18 and a senior in highschool. Immediately, he started to talk to me. "We should go out on a date." He said after a couple of days of endless flirting back and forth. I had never really had a boyfriend before. I was so nervous that I blurted out a quote from my favorite tv show. "Sure, pick me up at 8 and don't be late." I said giggling hoping he knew that I was quoting something from a tv show. I don't know why I thought that he would think me cool if I said stupid shit like that, but I did. He paid no attention to me. If he did know it was from a tv show he showed no recognition. His dark black eyes seemed to swallow me whole as he looked at me. He had a dark aura about him and somehow that little voice in the back of my head that should have warned me to stay away from him was enthralled as well.

To be honest, I didn't think he would show up. I wasn't exactly popular and at that time I thought of myself as extremely ugly. My mother would constantly tell me I was fat or ugly to the point where I had no self esteem at all. That Thursday right at 8 there was a knock at my front door. I was busy standing on a chair to see on top of the fridge for some benadryl. My allergies were killing me since a bush I was very much allergic to grew right outside the main school entry doors. All the other doors to the school were locked forcing me to have to hold my breath and run as fast as I could inside. Surprised and suddenly remembering the date, I fell off the chair. I clattered to the floor landing hard on my hip. I wanted to lay there stunned and not saying a word but I could feel my mother's eyes boring a hole in my skull. She was already in a bad mood for whatever reason so I didn't say a word about how my hip was now throbbing with pain. Carefully I got off the super clean floor. She was super strict and made sure I did above and beyond my chores. I remember one night she came home in a bad mood and her high heels stuck to a small drop of syrup on the floor. She got pissed off and wretched the high heel free smacking me upside the head as I scrubbed the floors with a toothbrush that was losing its bristles.

My mother looked at me with a disapproving glance before she got ready to leave. I never asked my mother where she was going, I knew better and didn't want the answer. I quickly explained why he was standing at my front door trying not to look impatient. "I am so sorry mom, I told him I would go out with him because I quoted from my favorite tv show. I didn't think he would actually show up!" I was nervously twirling my hair around my finger so tight it turned purple. "Can I go please?" I whispered. I could feel my heart beating loudly in my chest like an old engine.

"Whatever." My mother sighed as she carefully applied some makeup to her face. My mother was drop dead gorgeous and applied just enough makeup to the point where it didn' look like she had any on. I grabbed my purse with my cell phone and keys, clutching them tightly to my chest. "Thanks mom." I whispered. She grunted and nodded a little bit before she slipped on her high heels. Whenever she went out, she looked like she belonged in a ball thrown by rich people. She always wore a beautiful dress and high heels. She wore her hair pulled back into a simple bun that made her eyes look like steel wool.

"You look pretty tonight." I tried to smile but my heart was beating way too fast in my chest. "Thank you, be home by 10 please. You will need to watch your brother." She had curtly said before she was gone leaving behind just a hint of perfume. I checked on my little brother who was fast asleep and locked all the doors. I stepped out into the cool breeze that almost seemed to take my breath away. My t-shirt clung to my already developing chest making it skin tight. "Woah! You look amazing!" Jason breathed. He smelled of coffee and hair gel. I couldn't really see his eyes in the dark in the right lighting, he looked almost demonic.

I felt uncertain of what to do with my hands so I simply shoved them into my pockets. "What are we going to do?" I asked, trying to take a deep breath to settle my nerves. "Tonight, you will join me with some friends." He motioned to a convertible that was beat up a little bit. I got into the convertible but it was small and before too long we were both clinging to each other in the backseat. Whomever was his friend that was driving was a horrible driver and scared me a little bit. I thought for sure I was going to fly out of the car around some of those corners. He drove way too fast and reckless as he laughed loudly. I felt like I had gotten in the car with the joker from the batman movies. Gravel kept flying all over the car and landing in the back seat. A couple of pieces of gravel actually pelted me in the head from another turn that set the car on two wheels for a split second.

"Relax, I got you." He whispered as he pulled me tighter. I tried to smile but instead I got kissed. The first kiss was a bit sloppy thanks to sliding around a corner, but the second kiss took my breath away. I am surprised we didn't get the cops called on us for joyriding inside the city limits. We kept kissing throughout the entire cruise to the point where his friends were whining about us getting a room. Jason winked at me and made me blush. My alarm on my phone went off and I told them it was time for me to go home. Everyone in the car started to whine about how they were surprisingly having fun with me. I shook my head, it didn't matter. They were either going to take me home, or I was going to have to sprint home. My mom was not someone to be trifled with. It didn't matter if she was home or not, she always knew if I was late. I had time limits for everything and if I were even a nanosecond late there was hell to pay. Each punishment got more creative and cruel.

Eventually I was driven back home, however I was almost an hour late. I kept trying to get out of the car and Jason had a death grip on me to the point where I couldn't move. Thankfully my mother was not home to punish me. My mother was extremely strict when it came to punishing me. My knees knocked together loudly as I got out of the convertible. "Hey, Abby, can I see you again?" Jason yelled from the car. I giggled, blew him a kiss and yelled "Of course!" I ran back inside suddenly feeling like I couldn't breathe. I had spent the entire night with a guy who was legitimately into me. I checked the house to find my mother still gone and my brother sound asleep. I quietly changed into my pajamas that were silky and laid down thinking of my date. I didn't have a bed then so I was curled up into a small ball on the hard concrete floor that used to be part of the front porch. The concrete was beyond cold and was making my teeth chatter loudly. I didn't care, I was on cloud nine. I had spent a good portion of my life with an abusive home life as well as an abusive school life. I had spent my entire life hearing about my flaws to the point where I had no self confidence. It didn't even really occur to me the age difference. For once in my life, I felt like I was someone special.

So I dated Jason for a few months and then things started to slowly change. He talked to his buddies more than he did me. My insecurities became unraveled and I began to really try to be a better girlfriend. "I don't know what you want me to do for awhile. I am new at this sort of stuff." I hated sounding like a little kid.

He just sighed, "You don't want to know. Maybe it's just better if we break up." He said with his voice cracking. "What on Earth are you talking about?" I asked, making him look me directly in my eyes. My mother always said I had creepy eyes because they would turn colors according to my mood.

He glared when he was hiding things. So, he glared at me and I glared back. "Look, you are just too happy! I can't be with someone so plastic." He angrily said as he brushed past me making my shoulder hit the lockers. I stood there massaging my shoulder. What the fuck was he talking about? Is there such a thing as being too happy? Too happy to the point of being broken up with? I didn't really know, and I was back to feeling like I was worse than dirt.

Chapter 2

I paused to see Lollie intently staring at me over her cup of coffee. "Have you enjoyed my story thus far?" I asked her as I poured myself another cup of coffee. I checked my watch, satisfied I still had plenty of time to finish my story. I fished around the desk and looked up to see Lollie holding up my secret pack of smokes. "Looking for these doll? Does Mortimer know you smoke?" She asked as she threw the box at me. "Nah, but then Mortimer doesn't know that I am a secret bounty hunter that punishes everyone who has ever hurt me. He most definitely doesn't know that I smoke. He is perfectly fine not knowing." I laughed, tucking a strand of dark red hair behind my ear.

We sat there in silence for a few minutes. "How do you keep it all secret?" Lollie asked as she turned another page over of the printed conversation. "If he asks, I work in a big fancy office in the city as a stock analyst." I laughed. I really did love

Mortimer, he made me happy for the first time in my life. However, I couldn't tell him what I had been doing for the past 10 years, a part of me knows he wouldn't be able to handle it. He was such a peaceful person, any sort of violence would probably scare him. He knew the image I portrayed to the world but not the real me. I had been with Mortimer for almost 15 years now, and he never did question anything. At one point, he had said whatever I had done in my past, was my past. He was only interested in my present. "Are you two ever going to get married?" Lollie asked as I lit my cigarette. "I don't think so, I mean we have been together for 15 years now. He had popped the question at year 4 although he didn't do it in a sweet romantic way. I said yes, then nothing ever happened." I never let Lollie see how much that irritated me.

Sensing that was a sensitive subject for me she quickly went back to reading. I had printed out at least a 1000 pages of conversation for her to go through. Whenever we took anyone down, we always made sure of all the details. She used a long slender finger and pointed to something on the page. "What does he mean here?" I glanced over and went pale. "That is why he is going to Mitch. He wanted to see me naked because he is pretending to be an artist. Let me remind you, he thinks I am an 8 year old girl." I was trying not to lose my cool. "I am going to continue my story. You gotta know the entire thing." I whispered, taking another drag off my cigarette.

It took me a second to continue on with my story. My chest felt tight and my head felt like it was swimming. "Sorry, this is a really emotional story for me. I have been waiting for this for twenty years now." Lollie gave a small nod while she went back to reading the materials I had put in front of her. "This guy is making me sick. It will probably clear your conscience to tell me everything. I want very badly to give this guy to Mitch after reading some of the things in this transcript." I could tell there was fire in her eyes even behind the glasses. I lit another cigarette and checked the time once more. I don't know why I kept checking the time, I had four days before I was to meet Mortimer. Four days to wrap up this final adventure before I retired for good. I was hoping deep down inside that I could handle being just a nobody housewife, even if we didn't get married.

Chapter 3

Things in highschool were tough. I kept winding up dating Jason, it was almost like I had no willpower when it came to him. We would date, then he would make up some sort of excuse to break up with me. Eventually, things went south. I was running an errand for my mother between my shift at work. I had started working when I was 12 and was required to pay rent. I grew up in a very strict household, sure I was smart, but I needed more skills to survive the real world.

I had to buy my own food, school supplies and everything else in between. I worked full time and went to school full time while I took care of my littlest brother. Jason and I had been fighting an awful lot around that time. I was 15 maybe when we started to sleep together, and as soon as we did he completely changed. So there I was with my arms full of all the things my mother wanted me to get on my errands and he drove up.

I was in no mood to deal with him on that day. I put everything in the front passenger seat of my car and walked over to the driver side. "Where are you going?" He asked with his black eyes glittering at me. "Home." I said and opened up my car door. I was about to slide in when he pinned me up against the car. "Hey, you are having a bad day, and I am having a bad day let's get married." He whispered. He smelled of rotten onions and alcohol. I was stunned. We had broken up yet again, and there he was putting a very simple engagement ring on my bony finger. I nodded, and hopped into the car to drive off. He stood there watching me drive off with a confused look on his face. As soon as I got back to the house, he had texted me. "Was that a yes?" I didn't want to make him mad so I replied that it was. I wasn't really thinking about marrying him, but if it shut him up I would agree to it.

My mother was so very angry at me that day when she saw the ring. I got hit with a hairbrush until my skin split from the more deeper bruises. She hit me must have been way over a hundred times. She ended up breaking the brush on my back and a piece of it embedded itself actually in my spinal cord. She got dressed up nicely, and stormed out of the house. My brother was spending the night with a couple of his buddies down the street, so it was just me in the house. I locked myself in the bathroom and did my best to rip out the piece of hair brush out of my spine with a rusty pair of pliers. I couldn't find a pair that wasn't rusty to be honest, I didn't spend much time looking for it.

I bled all over my clothes as I cried in a tight ball on the floor. I wouldn't dream of bleeding all over my mother's floors, so I had no choice but to bleed all over what little clothes I had. I couldn't stand the thought that my mother was beginning to hate me so much. I picked up my clothes from the floor and slowly peeled them away from my swollen back. I quickly got dressed, I was down to three outfits outside of work clothes. I knew that I was going to have to pull extra shifts in order to get more clothes. I limped to the kitchen and gathered up the rest of the trash. There wasn't much trash since I took it out every day, but enough to hide my clothes. I had a sneaking suspicion my mother would go through each bag of trash if she had the time.

I spent a couple of days throwing myself into my work. I worked 16 hours straight just not to be home. I offered to cover shifts for a couple of people who called in. I could hardly move without wanting to scream but somehow I managed to pull through. I went home and slept for a couple of hours while my mother was out. I was getting bullied at school because I had to shop at a local thrift store. No one understood I couldn't afford nice clothes. My mother and father were fighting more. Each night a knock out drag out fight would happen. The air was filled with them screaming and hitting each other. The police were called almost every night. I didn't hardly see Jason much, there was no way he would even understand what I was going through.

When I did see him between all the craziness in my life that I viewed as normal, all we did was fuck and fight. At that point in my life, I just wanted to escape from it all. We never actually talked about the wedding and he never mentioned it again after the ring was on my finger. Things at work got bad because of a manager belittling me in front of everyone. Once the rest of the shift saw him doing that to me, everyone joined in. I couldn't catch a break.

Winter hit, and hit harder than ever. There was a massive snow/ ice storm that came through. People were without power for almost a week straight. The town was under a blanket of ice, and I got real sick. My car broke down in the garage, and seeing how my parents fought all the time, there was no way I was going to ask either of them for help. I was walking everywhere. Jason, couldn't care less to be honest. He barely noticed any of the hell I was enduring. Just like everyone else in the world, I had everyone all fooled.

After about 18 hours of my shift, I was walking home. I could barely make my body move and it started to snow even harder. I slipped on a patch of black ice. I landed hard on my foot and heard it crunch from underneath me. I still couldn't move even after it started to ice again. I just closed my eyes, I was cold sure, but at least it was quiet. No one was out at that time of night. The only thing I could hear was my teeth chattering, but after a while even that stopped. I don't know how long I lay in the street, or how I ended up in the hospital. I woke up underneath a mountain of warm hospital blankets. A tired looking nurse looked at me and smiled. "Welcome back. You have walking pneumonia, a broken foot, and you are severely dehydrated. You also look like it's been a while since you have had anything to eat. So here is a menu from the hospital cafeteria, order anything you want." I couldn't stop shivering and tried to grasp the menu. "You need to eat something honey. Otherwise, I'll have to start another IV in your arm for nourishment."

I ordered a cheeseburger and some french fries, then fell asleep while waiting on my food. I was alone in the hospital when my food arrived and by the time I woke up, it was cold. I managed to choke it down the best that I could. No one came to visit me in the hospital, and the only one who talked to me was that nurse. I only saw her one time and the rest of the time I spent dozing.

Eventually, I ripped out my IV and quickly got dressed. I had managed to make it out of the hospital without anyone noticing I was gone. I came back home to a whirlwind of hell. Jason and my mom were arguing. My brother had locked himself in my room so I couldn't get in it. I sent Jason home and faced my mother.

The next thing I knew, she slapped me hard across the face. "You are to never see that piece of shit ever again!" She screamed in my face. She didn't care that I was on crutches, or that I had been gone for several days. No one did. Not even Jason.

I walked to work and worked a 14 hour shift. I didn't want to go home so I walked to the school which was about four miles away and broke in. It was easy to do at that time, I knew the weight lifting room always had an unlocked window. I crawled in and fell asleep in the library. I waited out the storm at home, then I walked home. By the time I got home, my foot was swollen to the size of a basketball. I had to literally cut my shoe off of my foot. Jason came by while everyone was away, and instead of talking to me, he just ripped my clothes off. He didn't even ask, he didn't even check to see if I was in the mood for sex. "Maybe it's time you worked out, you are getting fat." He said in disgust. He got what he had wanted then left yet again. I was beginning to hate him. What sort of boyfriend does that? What sort of person is totally oblivious to the condition I was in. I barely weighed 80 lbs!

I traded my car in for another one because I was tired of walking everywhere. I had managed to lemon rig my previous car to where it at least started and ran for a brief time. At that time, they didn't really have any lemon laws. I merely just did what the dealers did at that time.

I wasn't feeling well so I went to the doctors. They checked out my foot and that's when I found out I was pregnant. I left the doctor's office and went to the lake to cry. I cried until my head hurt and there were no more tears. My life was over with, as soon as my mother would find out, she would kill me. She started to drink heavily and was gone for weeks at a time. I went to the gas station and bought some cigarettes. I knew the clerk so even though I was underage, she still sold them to me.

I went back out to my car and saw Jason with his arms wrapped around one of my friends. She was younger than I was, but way more sluttier than I could ever think to be. I watched him pull her close and kiss her then both went into the gas station. I was so pissed off that I threw my car in reverse and without looking drove into traffic. For a brief moment I was clear until a car sped up and hit me right on the driver door. I was flung out of the windshield and onto the road. The driver felt bad and called an ambulance for me. He even stayed right there in the street making sure I kept breathing. Jason glanced at the wreck and left with my friend.
I was taken to the hospital and the doctor was nice enough to not tell my mother I was pregnant. I lost the baby and suffered

from broken ribs. I went home and called Jason. "We need to talk." I said hoping he would come by. It took him four days to come over to talk to me. "I was in a bad car accident and I was pregnant. I lost the baby because I went through the windshield. I saw you kissing my friend, Jaimy." I was trying not to let him see me cry. He shrugged, and all he said was "So that was why you were getting fat."

He left just in time. Both of my parents showed up pissed off at each other. Another fight broke out, this time however, I got dragged into the middle of the fight. "You are late on rent young lady!" My father screamed at me. He ripped off his belt and it made an evil hiss as it escaped his belt loops. He started to hit me as hard as he could. I could feel the flesh on my back and legs start to crack. Hot blood rushed down my back as he continued to beat me. My mother had the time to finish off an entire bottle of everclear, and when my father got tired, she joined in.

They beat me for almost two hours. My bruises had bruises, my flesh looked like it had been filleted right off my back. You could see my pale grey bones from my spine poking through what mess was left of my back. "Get the fuck out of the house and don't you ever come back, you ungrateful bitch!" My mother screamed at me. Police showed up, and I managed to grab a couple of backpacks full of my stuff before I was hauled out of the house.

Once again, no one noticed the horrible abuse done to me. I had no place to go, no money and was still sick with broken bones. I threw what little I was able to grab into my car and drove straight to Jason's house. "I got kicked out, I need a place to stay." I said hoping he would notice something was wrong. "You can't stay here." He said in a cold voice. I threw my engagement ring at him and watched as the tiny diamond cut him in the face.

Chapter 4

I had to pause on the story, because I had started to cry too hard. "Sorry, Lollie, this is a really hard story to tell." She didn't say a word as she handed me a tissue. I dried my eyes and took a deep breath. "Let's order some food." Lollie suggested. I nodded, food actually sounded great. I waited patiently for Lollie to use the app to order us some food. "I never knew what you went through. I am so sorry you had to bear it. The good thing is somehow, you managed to work with me. You are the closest thing I have to a friend." Lollie said, wiping away more of my mascara that had smeared all over my face.

"Tonight, you will actually get to know the entire story of how and why I ended up working with you." I smiled. I gave her a quick hug. The doorbell sounded and she went to go pay for the food. "Ugh, it was the nasty looking delivery guy this time." She giggled as we divided up the food.

We sat there eating like we hadn't eaten in months. The food was hot and delicious. I was beginning to feel better and slid a bag by Lollie. "Here, go ahead and see your prize." I said tucking my long dark red hair once more behind my ears. Lollie's face lit up and began to anxiously dig around the bag. "There is almost a million dollars in here!" She whispered. Her eyes were wide from amazement. "Told you, the last one will pay the best." I laughed.

"Hello retirement in the Bahamas!" She giggled. She hugged me once more. I was really going to miss her, we had been working together for ten years now. "Let's finish the story and read all the transcripts then we can go hunting." I said sadly. "Are you sure you can finish?" She said as she settled back down in her chair. I nodded, "I have to. I have to be able to close this chapter in my life for good. You have to know everything, because I am not just going to hand him over to Mitch. This one, I am going to personally see to it, he is suffering." I could tell that Lollie understood.

I settled down in my favorite chair and pulled my legs up to my chest. Lollie turned another page and I began to talk once more.

Chapter 5

Where was I? Oh yes, so I threw the engagement ring at him and it cut him on the face. He still has that scar today, although it's not as noticable anymore. I had no one, and no place to go. I was supposed to survive the rest of the winter by myself on the streets. I spent a lot of cold lonely nights wanting to give up.

That empty feeling that makes you feel like the entire universe hates you, it can really tear at you. That's where I was. I was beyond rock bottom, and no one cared. People would spit at me and call me names as I walked by. I walked a lot because it was the only way I could keep warm. I didn't even have any winter clothes. All I had was a t-shirt and a pair of thin pants that whistled when the wind would blow around me. You could see my ribs through my t-shirt. My face looked hollow like a skeleton. People would toss pennies at my face and yell at me to get a job or to stop drinking.

My car got broken into while I was sleeping in the back of it. I was severely beaten by a couple of guys wearing dark masks. Everything I had except the clothes on my body and my school work was stolen. To top it all off, my car stopped running so I no longer had any source of heat. I would sneak over to my mother's house when I knew no one was around. She had the locks changed so I literally had to break into my old bedroom. I would eat, take a shower and wrap myself up in every blanket I could find. I managed to grab a few more of my things, leaving nothing but furniture at my mother's house.

My father and my brother took off to Arizona because they were tired of my mother. I never saw them again. Rumor has it they were both in a horrible car accident. Because my mother was almost never home anymore, the house became a dirty mess. I didn't bother to clean it, I just made sure, she never knew I was in the house. I lost more weight, and stopped sleeping. I had a couple of relationships, but for some reason, Jason always found a way to destroy them. I graduated school and enrolled in college. I didn't really have any sort of direction and was working two jobs to pay for it. I think I just went just to be able to say that I had some education under my belt.

I basically was a ghost and I went for the heat. I didn't make any friends and nobody really knew my name.

One night after he had been drinking, Jason didn't recognize me and hit me. He thought he was hitting a drum, and I ended up with a handprint bruise on my ribs that matched his hand. I had been invited over to an old highschool friend's house one night after finals. There was a huge party, and everyone was drinking. I drank so much, I gave myself alcohol poisoning.

I was sick and tired of this world pushing me down. I was tired of hurting. I slipped into a really dark place and decided it was time to end it all. I became obsessed with dying. I tried everything, including drinking bleach, taking a bunch of pills, slitting my wrists and nothing worked. Somehow I was always found just in the nick of time. I even went out to the cemetery that was outside of town to die.

I ditched my car, put all my belongings in a storage unit, and crawled up to a gravestone that was damaged. I lay there talking to ghosts because I had no one else to talk to. I was found, and brought to the hospital, to this day I still don't know who found me.

As soon as the hospital staff turned their backs on me, I ran off. I was just drifting from house to house. I no longer cared what happened to my body. I experimented with drugs, with people, just about everything to numb the constant pain I was in. My mother showed up one night and grabbed me by my throat. "You are such a dumb ass! You do realize that your precious Jason had a bet going to see if he could take your virginity! You mean nothing to no one!" She was extremely drunk, and her eyes were heavily glazed over like a donut. She smelled of stale sex and tequilla.

"Mom, I haven't seen Jason in almost a year." I sputtered. She spit in my face and the next thing I knew, I was on the floor. Everyone in the house including my mother started to hit me. I woke up to Jason putting me in an industrial trash bag. I couldn't move or even make a sound, I could tell there was a lot of damage done to my body this time. I wasn't even sure what they were hitting me with. Jason and his buddies hauled me to a drainage ditch that was right outside town and threw me in. I hit my head hard against the grate as I splashed to the waters below. The water smelled foul and was icy cold.

I no longer wanted to die, I wanted revenge. Why should they all get a great life while I am being kicked around like a dog? I let the water carry me away for quite some time. Every part of my body hurt, but somehow the water made it feel almost better. I crashed up against a sharp jagged pipe. I don't know how I managed to wretch my body free from the pipe, but I did. I was bleeding everywhere and I could feel my heart slowing. "Please, I don't want to die. They must pay." I whispered as my vision started to swirl with black spots. Pieces of the trash bag clung to my body causing me to slip every time I tried to move. Bones were sticking out all over my body to the point where I looked like a pinecone.

The blood in my head seemed like it was pulsating against my skull and my breaths became hard shudders. "Please." I whispered weakly. I had spent 3 years and almost 14 times trying to die. I had a purpose in life, and I didn't want to die this time. My blood had congealed making me stick to the hard concrete I clung to. I became a human pudding because of the blood and trash bag.

"What would you give to live and seek your revenge?" A male voice sounded. "Everything." I whispered. I didn't bother to try and find the voice, I was more concerned with trying not to choke on my bloody breath. "Done." He had said. I felt his warm calloused hand on my forehead. "You will live, your revenge you shall have. Your price is that you will belong to me." My forehead started to feel like it was stuck to a raging hot stove top.

He lifted me up by my arm and I heard my skin crackle from under his. I looked at my arm and realized he had branded me with a symbol. I didn't care. I waited patiently for him to heal me entirely, then injected me with a glowing purple serum. I never did see his face or get his name. To this day, I still don't really know who I sold my soul to. I honestly, just didn't care. The first person on my list was my mother.

I had endured years of abuse from her ever since I was born. I thought about her and the other people I wanted to add to my list as the man continued to help me.

It was weird hearing all my bones snap back together like they were made from legos. I didn't put much thought into my plan for my mom. After what seemed like hours he slipped a heavy key around my neck and whispered my instructions for my revenge. Then he was gone and I was able to rip off the trash bag. My clothes were bloody and dirty but I couldn't care less. It took me a while to figure out where I was so it felt like I walked around for hours. Eventually I saw the part I remembered being thrown in.

 I wandered back to her house and sat there on the grimy floor waiting for her return. I stayed in that house for almost two weeks before she finally showed up.

She didn't see me at first, she came into the house and took off her high heeled shoes. She sat down in her favorite chair that no one was ever allowed to sit in. Even if the house was filled with guests, no one was allowed to sit in her chair. I remember she had made our family from Honduras sit on the floor so not to sit in her chair.

Once she got comfortable, she started to rub her aching feet. "Hello mom." I said as I stepped out of the shadows. She didn't bother to say anything. She acted like I wasn't even there! It pissed me off that she didn't register that I was there. "Look at me!" I yelled at her. She actually yawned. "What do you want? You better not be here to borrow money!" She rolled her eyes.

"Borrow money? Are you high? I have never been able to borrow money from you!" I said trying not to show her how upset I was becoming. She stood up and glared at me. "Why are you here?" She said poking me in the shoulder. At first I couldn't find the words to say anything. She was still my mother, and I had forgotten how pretty she was. My chest tightened as I tried to breathe. "Why did you hurt me my entire life? Why did you hate me?" I managed to whisper.

She just shrugged. "Everything you did was such a disappointment. Especially when you got with Jason. I can't believe how dumb you are. I thought I raised you better than that." Her eyes danced with hatred. "Why did you care that I was with Jason, and that I turned out to be some bet?" I said inching closer. She laughed until tears started to roll down her face. "Because I was seeing him as well and lost the damn rent payment on the bet."

I didn't realize she was holding a knife and went into my ribs. It hurt but not in a way I had endured my entire life. I ripped out the blade and looked at the stringy piece of my flesh dangling from the tip of the blade. I put the tip of the blade in my mouth and slurped my flesh like it was a spaghetti noodle. "You are going to pay for that." I said no longer feeling the stab wound.

I admit I didn't torture her as long as I wanted to. I stabbed her in the head and tried to gut her in half. She died as the tip of the blade ripped through her throat. Just like what had been done to me, I put her in a trash bag. I sat there looking at the trash bag for a while breathing hard. I couldn't believe I actually took someone's life. I wanted to feel something, but I couldn't. I still felt empty.

I even rammed the knife into my leg just to feel something, but I felt nothing. I hardly even felt the pain as the knife embedded into my thigh bone. I sat there for the longest time just twisting the knife into my thigh. It finally dawned on me what I was capable of doing, what I had done. "Who needs a soul anyways?" I whispered to the trash bag.

I lit up one of my mom's smokes while I rummaged through her purse. Apparently, my mother was an escort. A very high end escort. There was a huge rolled up wad of cash along with a black book filled with her clients. Figures, my mother was a whore.

I blew another ring of smoke and decided it was time to burn this house to the ground. I poured gasoline on every inch of the place that was flammable. I poured extra on my mother to make sure the trash bag bonded with her dead corpse forever. I stopped in front of the mirror and put on a little makeup. Then I set the gasoline on fire and watched it burn from the garage. Once it got too hot to stand by, I slowly kept to the shadows and made my way out of town. I should have felt something about killing her, but hey, she was the first one on my list. I felt so powerful and I really hoped she was burning in hell.

Chapter 6

After I left town, there was a powerful feeling that was surging through my body. The brand on my arm burned and every time I crossed someone off the list, I felt powerful. It became more addictive than I could ever imagine. No drug could compare, not even the pain inflicted on myself didn't come close. I reached out to Jason a few times, because even though I knew what kind of a dick he was, I was still drawn to him.

My revenge took me all over the state and I have to admit I enjoyed every bit of it. I took care of everyone who ever hurt me except for Jason. For some reason, at first I wasn't able to bring myself to hurt him like he did me. Once that list was completely done, I took a knife and recarved the symbol on my arm. I made another deal. This time I was a bounty hunter going after really bad people. Once more I didn't see the man, but he gave me instructions to start feeding Mitch his "meals."

I can go into any prison and turn the key, it will take me right to his cell. Mitch will stay in that cell forever. He feeds off the people I put in his cell. He used to be alive like you and me. He had a daughter named Matilda and she died. She was kidnapped, tortured and killed. His own wife had sold her when she was only 14 years old. Mitch was in no condition to save her so he did a little black magic. He called forth a man to sell his soul to. To make sure no one would ever get away with hurting a child again, he made a deal. He got 19 souls already thanks to me, Jason will be his last. Then his deal is done, and so will mine.

Now, let me get to why I am giving him Jason. I spent years keeping track of Jason. We were together off and on, but it never worked out. He always found a way to hurt me, so then I would run off and find someone else to kill. I got addicted to pain, in a very bad way, because killing people stops being addictive. It was just another job to me, one I no longer took pleasure in. On my quest for revenge it put me in a bad way with a lot of bad people. At one point I was paying people to hurt me. In my own way, I became a pain whore, ironically.

I got married a couple of times and hated both husbands. The first one started to hurt me and almost succeeded in killing me. I added him to the list and made sure he knew what it felt like to be left for dead. I did check on him and the buzzards had picked his body clean. The second one, was completely whiny and a tool. I didn't kill him, I left him penniless on the streets wandering around talking to himself. The only good thing I got from him was my beautiful daughter. Abileen will be turning into a teenager this year. She is the reason why I decided it's time to retire.

I actually called Jason up hoping he would help me out. He said I deserved everything that happened to me. Then he crossed a line. He broke into my home and tried to take pictures of my daughter while she was showering. I beat the hell out of him but he ran off before I could give him to Mitch. It took me years to track him down. I decided it was time to settle down and take care of Abileen. I met Mortimer and instantly fell in love with him. He was nothing like anyone I had ever met. Then I met you and you have been amazing to help me on my quest. You helped me take down the ones I couldn't get to.

After some time, I got a tip from one of his "artist" friends saying he crossed a line with his daughter too. She was four and he tried to lure her away. I went online and posed as an 8 year old girl hoping to be tutored for school. All that you are reading is what we've been talking back and forth for the last three weeks. The time is perfect to end this. It's my birthday in four days. Mortimer, Abileen and myself are going to take a camping trip to celebrate. The best birthday present to me is knowing that piece of shit is suffering.

Chapter 7

Lollie sat there with her mouth open wide. "Wow, that's a hell of a story. You are a survivor from hell." She giggled at the pun. "Can I see your branding on your arm?" She said pushing her glasses back up her narrow nose. I nodded and slowly rolled up the sleeve on my shirt to show off the now gnarled scar. It was deep and took a good portion out of my bicep. It was a purplish green color that snaked to my shoulder. I had gotten a little carried away with recarving it.

"When we find him, I need you to grab a few things from his house. There is a box that he keeps under his mattress that's labeled as biohazard. That has everything in it I need.We will be taking him to a loft I rented under a different name so I can "prepare" him for Mitch." I said twirling my hair. Lollie nodded and took off her glasses. She carefully folded them and put them in her desk. "Not a problem." She sat there quietly for a while tapping at the keys on her laptop.

I closed my eyes. I couldn't believe I was going to be able to close this chapter of my past forever. I felt joy and that was something I hadn't felt except for when I had Abileen. I was ready for a normal and quiet life. This would complete my contract for my soul and I would be able to live out my days with the family that loves me. I was so lucky to have Mortimer and Abileen. If I didn't have them, who knows where I would be today.

Lollie sucked in her breath loudly and I opened my eyes. "I found him. He is working at a build-a-bear workshop at the mall 40 miles from here. What a sick bastard!" Of course the pedofile would be working there. I rolled my eyes. "Ok, you go ahead and apprehend him. Bring him to the location. I am going to go get ready and put on my skimpy cop outfit." I said crushing a lit cigarette in my palm. "Why do you wear that?" Lollie giggled as she stood up. "Because men are pigs and no matter the age, they like a good leg." I smiled. My heart was beating loudly in my chest.

Lollie packed up all the paperwork and her laptop into a small bag. She grabbed the bag of money as well, "Ok see you soon." She winked. I winked back and began to gather up my things as well. This would be the last time I would be in this office, and it had to look like I was never here.

I put on my skimpy cop outfit and waited patiently for Lollie. The loft was nice and secluded, as well as sound proof. It was only used for special occasions like this one. There was one particular room I personally designed to carry out my missions. It was made entirely of steel and had a variety of any sort of tool I could imagine. There was a nice big TV mounted on the wall as well as an intercom speaker on the walls. I could have a person locked in that room and host a dinner party, all the while neither party being aware of each other. No one would be able to find the room just stumbling about.

PART 2

Lollie was gone for only an hour. She must have sped the entire way there. She wheeled him on a dolly used for moving into the darkened loft. "I took a page from the movie Hannibal because the bastard tried to bite me." Lollie said.

Lollie always amazed me at her strength for being a couple of feet shorter than myself. I stood up from the chair I was sitting in and slowly came into their view. "Very well done Lollie. You know what to do next. Enjoy your retirement!" I smiled.

Lollie nodded, gave me a quick hug, handed me the box I asked for, then ran out of the loft saying into her walkie that the suspect she was chasing shot himself. I waited until I heard the door latch and lock from the outside then turned my attention to Jason.
"Hello Jason. It's been a while." I said softly. I wheeled him to the room that had no windows and left him against the wall. His eyes were bulging with desire as he watched my body sway. My body was toned slightly but filled with scars.I had lost count of the scars on my body but I didn't care. The scars were my reminder of indulging too much in pain. Guys dig the scars though, some have said it pulls their attention to me like a moth to a

flame. This proved to be true with Jason, his eyes continued to follow my scars as I swayed towards him.

"It's taken me many years to find you." I said sitting down on the stool in the room. I opened the box that Lollie had given me. The first thing I pulled out was a stack of ids. "I see why it has been so hard to find you. You keep changing your name. Look at all these. Nathan Denton, Johnathan Wilson, Jason Devont, Jason Jackson. This one just says deadpool. Really?" I started to fling the ids at his face. "You used a different id, probably a different personality for each one to be able to lure kids??" My temper was rising. I swallowed a small ball of rage from the back of my throat. I would not make the same mistake I did with my mother. I would make sure he suffered.

He mumbled something against the muzzle Lollie had put on him. "I am not going to take that muzzle off just yet. I don't need to know why you are a pedofile. Or why you betrayed me the way you did when you found out about Abileen? Or why did you not care anything about me, then on top of everything was seeing my friend AND mother behind my back? I loved you greatly and would have followed you to the ends of the Earth if you asked. I never meant anything to you, I was just a pawn in your sick twisted game of perversion. I kept running to you hoping you would help me. Instead you helped put me on the streets, and helped me sink into darkness." I shook my head and dug out a couple of other things out of the box. "Here is our prom photo. That's sweet, why on Earth did you keep it? You left me at the dance in order to go fuck my mother behind the building." I spat and ripped the picture into several pieces.

"Here is the ticket to my play I was in. I had spent nearly my entire paycheck to get a ticket to put you in the front row seat. You didn't even show up. You were too busy fucking Jaimy. You had meant so much to me that I used the money I needed for food to buy you that damn thing. I lost almost 20 lbs because of it. I even had to eat out of the dumpsters behind McDonalds for a while." I ripped up the ticket and threw it with the pieces of the picture. Jason had started to rock back and forth trying to free himself from the dolly.

"You better stop that and be still or I will start taking body parts off." I snarled. I was no longer worried about playing nice. There were a few folded up pieces of paper that were next in the box. "What's this?" I unfolded it and realized it was a story I had written in college trying to open his eyes to my hellish life. "You never bothered to read this story did you?" I asked, my eyes narrowing. He shook his head no.

I dug around the bench behind me until I came up with a bucket of industrial super glue. It was mainly used to keep trusses for houses in place. I poured the entire bucket over his head and watched as his body began to stick greatly to the dolly. His body loudly stiffened like it was being dipped in liquid nitrogen. "Good, now you have to listen." I smugly smiled. I used some tongs to peel back his eyelids so he could see me. The tongs got stuck and I tried to rip them off of his face. Both of his eyelids came off with the tongs leaving nothing but gaping bloody holes on his face.

Then I grabbed two icepicks and gently cleared out the glue from his ears. I made two holes where his nostrils were so he could breathe then settled back down on the stool.

"There we go! All better now." He looked so helpless and ridiculous I had to laugh.

"It would seem you are now in a sticky situation." I laughed.

****

I began to read out loud making sure I kept an eye on Jason while I read.

This is the story about Brandon and Amy.

Brandon and Amy lived next door to each other since they were

little.Since day one Brandon and Amy were best friends. Every

Brandon pledged his friendship and love to Amy. Brandon made

Amy a heart friendship necklace for valentines day and whispered

in her ear" One of these days I am going to marry you!"

As Brandon and Amy grew up their friendship grew also.

Amy found that she loved Brandon, but was a little afraid to

tell him. Brandon on the other hand only thought of Amy as one

of the guys and thought little about love. Every time Brandon got

himself into trouble Amy was there to help him out. She always

made sure that suicide was never an option for him. But as the years

progressed Brandon became uninterested in spending time with

Amy. He was too busy chasing his "dream" girl. Amy however

never gave up on him.

Amy would invite him to every function that she had, parties,

plays, dancing and even invited him out to dinner. She knew deep down

inside that he would come up with some lame excuse not to be there.

Then Brandon did a complete 360 change. He became very bitter and

cruel. He made Amy cry almost every day by his snide comments or

setting her up to take his falls. Soon those invites only caused

Amy's heart to break more. There were a few times that if he had

had he been there he would have saved her from the pain.

After college Amy ran far away from Brandon. Brandon had become

savage to her and she didn't have any more tears to be shed. 15 days

before her 22nd birthday, Amy got shot by a crackhead that was

holding up a gas station. Brandon learned that after all these years

Amy had left him something in her will. Brandon went to her

funeral, as he went up to see her, the priest handed him a metal,

heavy box. Amy had wrote in her will that only he should have

this particular box and had a special key fastened around her slender

wrist for him.

All of her relatives were glaring at him and pissing him off. So he

decided to light up a cigarette in the funeral home and storm out.

Half-way to his car thoughts of what could be in the metal box ran

wild in his mind, and absently flicked his cigarette over his

shoulder. He went to his motel room and opened the box with extreme

nervousness. In the box were a few photos, a letter and the necklace

he had made for her. He started to read the letter out loud to himself.

"My dearest Brandon if you are reading this then something has

happened to me. I wanted you to know that every even that something

bad happened to me because you weren't there, I took a picture of.

Look at them closely. I have loved you ever since I met you, but in

in the end I was pushed the farthest away from you. You broke my heart

into a million pieces, and laughed as you stepped on my heart. Now

wipe those tears from your eyes, you never cared for me. So why start

now?"

He picked up the first photo with shaking hands. It was a picture of

a baby tied up to a high chair and the mother leaning over to untie

the baby. The mother's face frozen with silent agony. On the mother's bare back was an iron that was sizzling her flesh by a strong looking

man. Amy had written on the photo the words " The reason I moved

next door to you"

The second photo was taken at a play she begged him to come and see

but instead he spent the night talking to his current girlfriend. The

The picture was of her standing on a stage in a girlie looking outfit. On

her arms and legs were deep cuts that didn't look like it went with

the play. Amy had written on the photo " If you would have cared

enough to come you would have seen this"

The next photo was taken at a rave one he had promised to meet her

at.She was dancing in the middle of the floor with scary looking men all around her each with a weapon and a look of hatred. Tears started

to stream down his face, as he read her handwriting on the picture "

The night you said you would meet me there but never showed up"

The last photo wretched his heart from his chest. It was the new

year's eve party that his buddies held, he was late to it but went and

avoided Amy. The picture was her standing alone in the crowd,

she looked awful. There was a faint track mark on her arm, her ribs

showed thru her shirt. There was a handprint bruise around her

neck.She was holding an alcohol bottle in one hand, and a bottle of

rubbing alcohol in the other. on her wrist was an angry slash mark that was staining her pale skin crimson. The floor around her were littered

with pills bottles, all emptied.

At the bottom was another note to Brandon " You were so busy with

chasing your 'dream' girl that you didn't notice how depressed I got.

Every night you made me cry I fought like hell to stay alive. When we

were little I could always count on you, then something changed and

your heart became cold. I loved you so much that living that way I was

only killed me in the end. I couldn't live without you. You never

appreciated anything that I did for you, so Brandon dry your tears,

it's too late to be caring now.

Brandon sat back with tears streaming down his face. He remembered the nights he talked to her and her behavior was funny. She had been

cutting on herself and trying to kill herself. He remembered that she

had told him once what was going on but he only responded with ' It's

your choice, you are a big girl you can take care of yourself'.

Brandon jumped back in his car, and drove fast back to the funeral

parlor. He had to see her one last time before they buried her.

He got to the funeral parlor only to find it engulfed in flames. He

sat there dumbfounded. A quiet voice said beside him " It was your

cigarette that caused it, the nail on the coffin." He looked over to

see Amy's ghost sitting there before he could tell her how sorry he before she faded away. He drove to the cemetery and wept at her open

grave.

Brandon woke up screaming, his head pounding. He went over to his

mirror and looked deeply at his reflection unsure what the dream meant.

He looked around helplessly at his school yearbook, Amy didn't

exist in his school, or anywhere else in his life. In frustration he

slammed the book shut and went for a drive trying to find the girl in

his dreams. Just when he was about to give up he saw her standing

alone by a ruined wall. With his heart slamming into his chest he

stopped and jumped out. He rushed at her and gave her a huge hug.

Amy blinked not sure what to do with the strange man hugging

her. Quietly she stepped to the side of him and looked at him deep

into his eyes. Brandon was crying telling her about his dream, and her

heart warmed to him. She brushed away his tears and asked him if he

wanted to get out of the cold, grab a bite to eat. She knew better

than to trust strangers but there was something about Brandon that

called to her. When she was sitting right beside him sharing a giant

plate of fries she couldn't help but think she was complete.

Amy told the story of her life while Brandon nodded vigorously.

She showed him the marks on her arms that showed a suicidal defeat, and showed the scar by her chest that was the remainder of a

tremendous battle. Then Brandon did something that surprised her, he

took her arms and wept unto her scars causing them to heal up

completely and vanish.

Amy backed away frightened, "what are you?" she said in a

shaking voice. Brandon replied " I am not sure but I know I am here to

help you and keep you alive." Amy thought the man strange but

kept it to herself.

They spent the next few years protecting each other and being there

for each other that many had said that they were inseparable. However

Amy felt strange as the time progressed. She felt that Brandon

was only protecting her because of a dream he had. She didn't realize

how much he did enjoy her company or that he had began to fall in love

with her.

One night Amy had to leave town due to a sick relative, in the

haste she wasn't able to say goodbye to Brandon. Brandon spent the

next few weeks looking for Amy. Amy ended up getting into

a really bad car accident and slipped into a coma.

Amy had disappeared off the face of the Earth, and Brandon

didn't know what to do. He feared something had happened to her and he had failed her again. Brandon decided that Amy was worth more to

him than anything and called in a private investigator to track her down.

When Brandon found out she was in a coma, he rushed to the hospital

and sat there beside her talking to her. Everything he said she heard

and began to fight for her life.

However, late that night, Amy's past came and took Brandon away

from her. When she awoke the scar on her chest pulsed, and she knew

what had happened. She checked herself out of the hospital and went to

go find Brandon cursing herself that the person who gave her that scar

had returned once more.

She followed her heart, knowing that she was closer to Brandon just by

the way it was beating. When she got there she ended up fighting for

her life, not thinking he would understand why she was in this

situation again, she made a deal with the person who gave her that

scar. Her life for his, Brandon was let go after getting beat up by

the hired men and was ditched by the side of the road. However Brandon

kept fighting, trying to get Amy to safety.

Amy spent three years in hell constantly missing Brandon, and

every chance she got she would get into contact with him just to ease

his mind. At the end of the three years, Amy died a horrible, gruesome death. Her body was lay in an unmarked grave,and although

Brandon was never told he knew exactly what had happened. He felt that

life couldn't go on as he knew it, and shot himself in the head.

Miles apart both awoke screaming, and instantly knew they were meant

to be together. Amy vowed that she would get to the man in her

dreams and make sure nothing ripped them apart. Brandon screamed out

his rage from his dream to the night sky. In his dreams he was with

the woman he loved and even in his dreams she was taken away from him.

Wings ripped from his back as he transformed, and at that same moment

Amy transformed as well. Both became a legendary being with

extreme powers. In the night came the whisper " I love you and one of

these days I'm going to marry you."

To this day both Brandon and Amy scream their rage unto the

night sky, legend has it they are the exact pieces of a ying yang. The

only way for the two souls to be happy and go back to their human form

is with each other. Is this tale real you ask? I'll let you decide.

All legends are based on truth at some point.

"I wrote that story hoping you would read it and somehow make up for the shitty way you treated me. In my story I had written you as a hero, someone searching for love." I sighed loudly then began to rip the story in shreds. I put it with the picture, and ticket. I had a nice neat pile of ripped up paper. None of it mattered anymore, I no longer felt any sort of love for him. "Too bad, I didn't realize what sort of monster you would grow up to be."

"The last thing in this box is a ziploc bag full of pictures of children. Some are clothed, some aren't. Almost all are crying in the pictures. You really are a sick fuck. I know you are probably going to say that being a pedofile is natural these days and that there is nothing wrong with anything you are doing. Then you will probably say something like you need the pictures because you are an artist and want to be able to draw people the right way." I rolled my eyes. "I never believed you were a great artist. Most of the shit you drew in highschool looked like a blind left handed person drew it."

I put the pictures back in the ziploc bag. Those would go to Mitch when I got done with Jason. "I sold my soul to get rid of people like you in my life. You will be my last final cleansing act, the last closed chapter in my past. There is nothing you can say or do that is going to lessen your sentence. The rest of the world thinks you are a coward by shooting yourself as a cop chased you down. At this moment Lollie is making sure the contents of your laptop is being shown to the public. I can only imagine your poor fragile parents weeping. Your dad with triple by-pass surgery, your mom has her own bill of failing health problems. I can picture your dad saying something how you had everyone in the world fooled. I can see how his anger on how you ended up makes him disown you." I smiled.

I went over to him and slowly ripped off the muzzle off of his face. It took a few minutes to grasp the muzzle and pieces of long shreds of flesh came off with it. The shreds of flesh were hard as well as squishy underneath. Dark pools of blood appeared where the muzzle used to be. "I am sorry I was such a shitty boyfriend, but I am no longer that same guy." He mumbled. "Too little, too late! You tried to look at my daughter in a perverted way! You lured all those children from the pictures in that ziploc bag away from their homes!" I screeched. I didn't care how much he said he had changed, he was still a scumbag in my eyes.

I went to the bench and grabbed the canister that had Hiymalan salt in it. It had huge, coarse, pink grains of salt in it. It made steaks taste amazing but I found it was great for this sort of thing as well. I poured a handful and started to scrub where the muzzle used to be. I made sure I grinded as much of the salt that I could into his face. He was screaming shrilly and starting to drool out the side of his mouth. I poured another handful and started to rub his face harder than before. Tears splashed down his face as I poured the remainder of the canister in my hand. I did one more through scrubbing until his face looked like it had pieces of gravel embedded in it.

"Does it hurt?" I said looking deep into his black eyes. I used to get lost looking at them for hours, now I felt nothing. He mumbled something incoherently and a line of drool pooled on his chin.

"Are you thirsty?" I asked, faking a sweet voice. He mumbled something again but I wasn't paying attention to him. I poured a little bit of bleach and mixed it with some kool-aid. "When I kept trying to die, I actually drank bleach. I mixed it with a lemonade flavored kool-aid just like I have made for you. However, I am going to have to do some improvement so you can drink this from a straw." I put the cup down and watch the bleach swirl in the cup with small chunks. I picked up a drill and pretended his teeth was a screw I was screwing into a wall. His enamel made a loud cracking sound as the drill went deeper into his teeth. The drill started to smoke some and just as I broke through his teeth my phone rang.

"Hello?" I asked. "Hey, it's me Lollie. You might want to turn on the t.v." The phone went dead in my hands. It was strange she was calling me, after the job was done I normally didn't hear from her. "What have you done?" I asked Jason.

I turned on a tv and quickly flipped it to the news. The news reporter had finished interviewing Lollie who looked visibly sick on camera. "I chased the suspect into the drainage system and before I could apprehend him, he shot himself." I nodded, that was the story we had come up with. The camera panned to an old house with faded yellowing trim. "Police searched through Jason DeVon's place of residence and was shocked to find that this was more than just a drug dealer shooting himself." A heavy set cop who I knew as Baird came in front of the camera. "Upon searching his residence we found a skeleton under the bed. Further investigation and we are still uncovering bodies. The ages range anywhere from 4 years old to 40 years old and so far it's only been females. This man was sick and so far we have found 40 bodies. Cadaver dogs have been brought out, we are now thinking that the inside of the walls holds more. Four more bodies have turned up in the garden. That is all we know for now and as soon as we know more we will keep the public updated." Baird left the reporter and trudged back into the house.

"40 and 4. Terror404. That's your body count." I slapped him hard where chunks of salted flesh came off in my hand. He slowly tried to nod. "How did you know?"

He whispered. I got out the copies of the transcript and slammed them down in front of him. "Because for the last three weeks you have been talking to an 8 year old girl by the name of Preciousgirl8 which was me!" I shoved a metal straw into the kool-aid mixture I made and shoved it roughly into his mouth. I pinched his Adam's apple until he started to reluctantly suck out of the straw.

"That much bleach won't kill you, it's just going to make you really sick." When the entire cup had been sucked down, I slowly shoved the straw deeper into his mouth. His teeth cracked more under the force and soon I hit his uvula. I aimed the straw down and quickly rammed it into his throat. He had no choice but to swallow the straw and his teeth as well. I could see the straw slowly stick in his throat before sliding the rest of the way down.

Blood was running out of his stiffened face, but I didn't feel any sort of remorse. "Do you think you have been punished enough?" I watched him closely. I could tell in his eyes he believed so, and it made me laugh. "I could torture you until the end of time and it wouldn't be enough." I said coldly.

I dialed Lollie's private number once more. "Yea, I saw the news. I'll throw in more money if when I get done with him, you can sneak me into solitary. It will be easier to deliver him that way. Lollie, you are such a doll." I laughed. Lollie of course had no problems with sneaking me into solitary at the prison. We paid a couple of the guards to turn away anytime I showed up. Since I paid them handsomely it was never an issue as to why I led people into the prison, and how come they were never seen again.

A loud clatter echoed in my ears and I glanced over to Jason to see his entire body convulsing. He was shaking the dolly so hard with each convulsion. "Ah, that's the bleach kicking in. I better help clear your mouth so you don't choke to death on your own vomit. I grabbed a sledgehammer that had a metal spike customly put into the head. I swung it as hard as I could against his mouth. Teeth and facial bones cracked loudly. Hot vomit spewed out of his mouth sending his teeth flying like they were bullets out of a gun. Vomit and blood dribbled all down his clothes.

Chunks of his inside splashed loudly at the dolly's wheels. His mouth was completely caved in from the force of the sledgehammer. The metal spike had embedded itself into his nose and ripped the middle piece leaving a nasty jagged bloody line where it used to be. He was wheezing and sputtering heavily as he tried to breathe. I stepped out of the room for a second and called Mortimer. He was my rock and kept me going, and I didn't want my rage to consume me entirely before I was able to finish my task.

"Hi babe! I am out for lunch and just wanted to tell you I love you. I can't wait to be done, and retired in four days!" I squealed happily. I talked to him for a few minutes then hung up the phone. "Thanks to you, I found my true love. He would never harm me or Abilene. It is a good thing you were such an ass. You drove me right to him. Now I can't see my life without him, but I can see my life without you."

He was sobbing like a little kid making the glue on his face crack. Teeth were still cracking and falling out of his mouth. I grabbed some pliers, ironically it was the same rusted pair that I used on my back years ago. For some reason right before I set the fire at my mom's, I had kept them. I pulled out the rest of his teeth until his gums were nothing more than bloodied holes. I could see some small nerves pulsating in the gums slightly. "That must really hurt." I whispered to him. He was starting to look like a joker from the batman movies. Blood was everywhere. "You are looking too happy, and you have gotten fat." I said in a hateful voice.

I cut off his smelly clothes around the dolly straps. I would make him eat them later. I grabbed a piece of flab from his stomach and began to slowly cut it with some office scissors. The scissors were sticking a little bit almost like I was playing with playdough. "Fat, fat, fat, got to get rid of that fat." I sang as I kept cutting. I knew I wasn't doing much damage to his organs. I took the pieces of stomach I cut off and shoved them in his mouth. Once more I pinched his adam's apple until the skin around my fingers bruised. He was eating his own stomach fold and gagging on it. I couldn't stop smiling, his pain was euphoric.

"All the pain I have inflicted on you, is exactly what I felt like while I was dating you. You were my first love, my first boyfriend and I was only a bet to you. Someone you could get to date you so you could fuck my mother. My mother, the high end whore of all things. Now we are even for what you have done to me. It's time to be punished for everything you did to all the dead you caused! Time to punish you for all the children."

I lit a cigarette thinking hard about what I wanted to do. It would feel too easy if I just dismembered his penis. I wanted him to suffer, and live through it all. He was dry heaving and blubbering like an idiot. I picked up the blowtorch and turned it on. First I touched his exposed stomach to it just enough to where the wound was bubbling like cheese melting on a pizza. His burning flesh was starting to smell pretty horrid, and I was hoping that was because he had contracted some sort of std. I was hoping that acrid smell that normally burning flesh doesn't smell like was because of that.

He was screaming with more blood and spit flying out of his mouth. Next I touched his gums with the blowtorch. Pieces of his gums popped loudly like hot grease and left burnt holes in his mouth. I was able to see his bones in his mouth. I kept the blowtorch on his gums until the bone was starting to melt a little bit. "There, now you won't bleed to death, can't have you dying when the fun is just starting to happen."

"Where you are going you are not going to need much." I said laughing. I kept the news playing in the background as I grabbed up some garden shears from the bench. I slowly cut off seven out of ten of his fingers, then I touched the blowtorch to each stub. Some of his skin had bubbled up and started to turn a greenish black around the wounds, like burnt sausages covered in mold. His flesh was really giving off a bad stench and I started to gag. Why on Earth did he stink so badly? I had burnt a few people on my quest for revenge and none of them smelled this bad. I couldn't help it and hot, sticky vomit spewed out of my mouth all over his face. Chunks of my delicious dinner were stuck to his congealed blood. I wiped my mouth with a rag then decided it was time to do something more. He had taken pictures of kids, which means it was time to do something to his eyes. I thought for a second then an idea hit me. I dug around in my bag until I got out my contacts. I dipped them into the bleach and kool-aid mixture I had left, then let them dry a little bit on some huge grains of salt. He had no eyelids, so it was easy to put the contacts on his eyeballs themselves. He let out a shriek that made me death as the contacts touched his eyes. His black eyes turned an icy red color and I could see every vein in his eyes. I took care of the eyes, and fingers it was time to take care of the evil within him.

"I don't know about you, but I am famished!" I had brought my lunch with me and was eating a huge cheeseburger in front of him. I made sure he could smell how delicious it was to the point where his stomach grumbled loudly. Weeks ago, I had put a vat of moldy food in the room with a metal lid covering it. I held my breath and dipped into the vat. I pulled out something that looked like it used to be a sandwich but was now alive with writhing maggots.

I pinched his Adam's apple until I thought it was going to pop from the force of my fingers. He opened his mouth to scream and I shoved the sandwich into his mouth. Blood and pus dripped from his eyes onto his check. His tears were making small holes wherever they lay. Maggots wriggled out of his mouth and began to feast on his mouth. One of the maggots actually snuggled itself in one of the holes in his gums. I dipped my hand in again and pulled out more food. I think it used to be maybe a salad or something. It was incredibly slimey. I kept shoving nasty, fuzzy, slimey and mold covered food into his mouth until his mouth was completely filled with maggots.

I finally let go of his Adam's apple and saw that it was turning black and blue. He was gagging as more maggots slid down his throat. I put the metal lid back over the vat and shook off any maggots on my hands onto his face. "It looks like some of your wounds have an infection. I should clean that!" I said brightly. I glanced at the t.v. and saw more bodies being brought out of the house under dark tarps. I pulled out a glass jar that had the biggest leeches I could find. I broke the jar over his head sending the acrid liquid and leeches all over him. He was crying and a couple of the fatter leeches landed in his mouth and latched onto his tongue.

It was time to take him off the dolly. I knocked the dolly off from the wall and began to disassemble the wheels. Once I got the wheels off, I began to slowly peel Jason off of the dolly. All of his skin that touched the dolly ripped away like an angry child pulling at a bandaid. I giggled at the thought of what Mitch was going to say when I gave him this one. He would be the first one that didn't have most of his skin.

I took the sledgehammer and broke his kneecaps. With each hit I did, I made sure the bone inside the knee cap turned to jelly. Then I broke both of his elbows with the sledgehammer. His knees and elbows looked like they were made from rubber. I flipped him over and set fire to him entire backside. I put it out as soon as it started to engulf him. I poured more bleach kool-aid down his back until all that was left was sizzling muscles.

I flipped him over and more insects went down his throat. I started to screw the wheels to the bottoms of his feet. Surprisingly, it was relatively easy to screw in the wheels. The glue on his feet made the skin nice and taunt. I kept screwing in the wheels until I could hear his bones cracking loudly. The bones gave me some resistance but I let my rage take over as I shoved the wheels further past the bones.

He was sobbing and trying to plead with me to stop. The more he opened his mouth, the more maggots slid down his throat. A leach had moved it's way to his eye and was sucking on his eye. The entire eye turned bright red, then milky white. I looked closer and found that the maggot had eaten a hole in the eyeball itself. Eyeball pus started to roll down his face.

With his elbows broken to the point where all the bone had shattered beyond repair, it was easy to literally tie his arms in a knot behind him. I flipped him over one last time. I poured more industrial glue down his back making his arms forever stick to what was left of his back. I flipped him back onto his back and watched chunks of his tongue slide down his chin as the maggots and leeches enjoyed their buffet.

I had one last thing I wanted to do to him. I took the rusty pliers and put them by his ballsack. I slowly moved it to where the ballsack actually was attached to the body. I pinched the skin ever so slightly and was rewarded with a wail. I smiled at Jason who was desperately trying to get away, but was failing miserably. "Oh, don't worry, I am not going to use those pliers. I just wanted to see how tender that spot is."

"Crazy bitch!" He mumbled as more drool slid down what was left of his face. "Tsk,

tsk, tsk, that is not very nice! You are the one who made the decisions, now you must face the consequences!" I dug around in my lunch box until I found some toothpicks. I rammed them as hard as I could right where the pliers were. It took a while of me ramming until the toothpicks actually pierced the skin. Each time I shoved toothpicks deeper inside of the small hole I made, he would wail like a hurt puppy. "Good, I am glad this hurts. You should have never hurt any kids in any way!" I screamed at him.

I glanced at the t.v. once more and stopped dead in my tracks. There was a body of a little girl that was being toted out of the house that I recognized. My little cousin, Claira, was a troubled teen that we all thought ran away. I recognized my favorite sweater that had come up missing. It now hung loosely on a corpse that was badly mangled. "You son of a bitch! You killed my cousin Claira??" I screamed and began to shove the entire bottle of toothpicks into his scrotum. I had shoved so many toothpicks in him that his balls actually broke free and dropped to the floor with a loud squish. I lit another cigarette and put it out on his bleeding ball sack.

I kicked him in the penis over and over again until the entire member was darkening with bruises. It was laying at a weird angle and looked like a severally over ripened banana. I sat there breathing hard, trying to collect my thoughts. "I fucking hate you Jason!" I screamed at him. I lit another cigarette. This one was really messing with me, it was supposed to be an easy revenge. I had no problems with torturing him or sending him to the devil in exchange for my soul. I had problems with what that man had done up to this point. How could someone be so vile and willingly destroy someone's entire world?

I picked up the balls and shoved them both into his mouth forcing him to swallow. I called Lollie, "Hey doll, I um, ready for you to let me into the prison." I sighed. She said it would be almost an hour before she could make a dash to the prison. I hung up the phone and stared at the broken and bloodied man on the floor. "It's going to be an hour before I can take you to your final place. I may as well tell you the story about Mitch." I could tell he wasn't listening much, he was too busy crying. He kept blubbering how he didn't care and that I was just a crazy bitch. I reached back into the vat and dug out more maggots. I covered his body with maggots then settled down to tell the story about Mitch. "Now, now you will listen to this story." I said in a cruel voice.

"Mitch was married to my sister, Katie, a very long time ago. He messed up and cheated on her. She went crazy and really fucked him up. Once things got bad for him he realized that she had a gambling problem, and the daughter he thought ran away, his wife sold to settle her debts. His rage landed him a deal. My sister had to pay the price just like my mother. I waited until she fell asleep, broke into her home, and doused her with her own favorite perfume. I set her on fire in her house. Mitch got a second chance but gets to rot in his own prison cell since his deal couldn't erase what my sister had done." Maggots were getting caught in the holes of his melted face. He was mumbling and crying which was irritating me. I grabbed an icepick and went to his mangled stomach. I started to repeatedly stab him over and over again with short jabs. I was creating a word from his collarbone to his waist. Pedophile. He was sobbing like a little girl and it made me laugh. "There this should shut you up!" I started to pour a little bit of the kool-aid I had left all over it. The skin started to bubble and crisp as the bleach sank deep into the tissues.

I lit a cigarette and blew the smoke into his face. He started to choke on the maggots and spewed blood everywhere. Luckily for me, I was sitting far enough away to not get any blood on me. "Now, where was I? The story about Mitch is really out there. However, if I have learned anything in this life, it's that there are things that can't be explained. There are things that don't make any sense to a rational and logical human being. Right before Mitch entered his last prison, he told me this story. The story was so chilling, I actually memorized it word from word. Now be good, and start eating those maggots while I am talking or I will do even more damage to you!" I watched closely as he slowly tried to gum some of the thicker maggots with where his teeth used to be. He looked scared of me which made me smile even bigger.

"Keep chewing! If I didn't know Mitch and his current predicament, I would think it was a bunch of bullshit." I decided that while I was telling this story, I would try to clean some of Jason's wounds. I really wanted to keep him alive long enough for Mitch to have his fun with. I took the koolaid bucket and sat it on the floor beside me as I roughly began to clean all the wounds slowly as I talked.

I took the shredded pieces of the prom picture and story from the table. I started to shove the pieces deep inside each wound until it hit bones.

Part 3
Mitch

Fear. Yes, that is what he felt. The urge to find a place to hide and fast, the fear of the pain he would endure. His loving wife was transformed into a blood hungry monster. Now she was just hunting him for sport and that thought scared him greatly. His wife was a great person until someone pissed her off, then all bets were off. Tonight she walked into the bedroom where she had caught him with the attractive neighbor down the street. He was pounding her doggystyle and so close to coming when he heard his wife gasp in surprise. Instantly he knew he was going to die. " Mellie get out of my house right this second before this becomes your final resting spot." His wife quietly said her eyes dancing dangerously. "Fuck,honey, I am so sorry. It wasn't what it looked like." "Save it!" she shouted at him, scaring him. Quietly he threw back on his clothes, and Mellie fled naked down the street."I should have known." she angrily hissed at him. There was no reasoning with her at this point, all he could do was grab his wallet and run.

Life as he knew it was over with, it was time to start over. He ran down the block and texted Mellie, "I'll be back for you." Before he could push the send button a shot rang out. Startled he turned around and tripped over a sidewalk crack. He landed hard on his elbow, which made him want to scream in pain. His wife stood elegantly in the middle of the road holding his shotgun in both of her pale hands. Another shot rang out, but this time she got his phone. It exploded into a million pieces. He could see Mellie running up behind his wife. "No! Mellie Don't!" he screamed, scrambling up on his feet. It was too late.

His wife swung around and took aim. Another shot but this time Mellie's head exploded all over the cars around. Her perfect body fell to the ground and crimson started to pool around her. "FUCK!" I screamed and took off running. One more shot and this one hit him square in the shoulder.

It was a pain he had never felt, or could even describe. It wasn't like the movies, it was painful. His wife jogged up beside him and pulled him up by his hair. She dragged him down the street and threw him inside the house. How is that neighbors weren't around to hear or see it all was beyond him.

"There is no escaping."His wife quietly said with a dangerous smile that played on her

face. She kicked him down the stairs into the basement. Then grabbed a hold of his shoulder making him scream out in pain. She proceeded to drag him to a part of the basement he had never seen before. Confused he started to struggle away from her, but she just laughed. There was a small handle on the basement floor that she opened, then kicked him down the short flight of stairs.

It was a small hole no bigger than the length of his body. The hole was made from smooth cold steel. "Where is this place?" he asked. "Oh I had this built the last business trip you made by yourself. I had a hunch I was going to eventually catch you cheating on me. I told you in the vows I didn't believe in divorce. At the time you just laughed, well you fucked up, welcome to the place where you will spend the rest of your life. There is no escaping." She said with what could only be described as joy. With that, she shut the door plunging him into darkness.

Chapter 1

The cold darkness was beginning to affect poor Mitch's mind. He couldn't remember what was real or even how long he was in the hole. His wife, Katie opened the hole just long enough to throw him handfuls of dog food. "Only dogs deserve dog food, not people food." She would tell him each time pelting him hard with the handfuls. At first he didn't eat it. This was ridiculous; she had to let him up eventually. But as time spun on and on he realized she had plans to do no such thing. Soon enough he had to empty his bowels and had no other choice but to go to the bathroom right where he was sitting. He was literally stuck to the metal from his own waste. He hung his head in shame, regretting everything up to this point in his life.

Chapter 2

"Whew! You stink, you pig!" Katie exclaimed opening up the hatch. "Fuck you." he sneered at her. "Wrong answer!" she laughed. She shut the hatch and he could hear her moving around the floors above him. He started shivering, *This is going to be bad.* He thought to himself.

Suddenly Katie yanked him up from the hole. She chained him to an old antique radiator heater. Then shackled his legs to the walls on each side of him. It's funny, he never noticed the hooks protruding from the walls.

Katie cut off his clothes and tossed them in a black hefty garbage bag. That's when he noticed the kitchen grade sink that had been installed while he was away. It had an industrial sprayer and stocked with plenty of chemicals that itself could be a bomb.

Katie laughed, "You like the newest additions? " She asked and started to spray him. His pale skin started to turn red from the force and heat. He just hung his head and did his best not to scream. Then she sprayed the hose in his hole that had become his new living arrangements. "I am going to have to think of something else for you, I don't want to have to keep hosing you down. Besides if I sew up your ass hole then you will die of sepsis within a week. Dogs don't get to die." She said in a sweet voice that sent shivers down his spine.

She went over to him and he head butted her in the forehead. "Why you little bastard!" she screamed, rubbing the new bruise that was forming on her forehead. You will pay for that!" and stormed off.

Mitch started to laugh quietly at first, but then loudly. It felt good to do her harm, and he wanted to harm her. He was so angry and missed Mellie. In his mind, Mellie was his perfect woman. Every night, he watched her brains splatter all over the road in a horrible nightmare loop.

He did a quick survey of the room taking in every new thing, memorizing every part. He would find a way to hurt her, he was going to kill her. But for now, he was enjoying not being in that damned hole even if he was still chained up. She came back in and watched as his slender wife started to yank up the steel from the hole. It fascinated him, he had no idea she was so strong. He had always just assumed she was fragile.

Once the floor was out, she started to dig some more. Then put a piece of pipe that resembled a gutter. He watched her in silence, this was a handy side of her he never saw. It actually was turning him on, and did his best to hide his hardened cock away from her sight with his body. She cut a hole in the steel then put it securely in the hold. On top of that she placed a small metal grate with jagged edges.

"Oh, you like that big boy?" she asked, turning around eyeing his member. "Fuck off." he said without thinking. Her face hardened and she grabbed some garden shears. She chopped off the tip of his penis with one quick fluent motion. "You bitch!" he screamed tears running down his cheeks. "Mmmmm." she started to suck on his cock lapping up the blood like it was water. Finally she grunted with satisfaction and seared it with a blowtorch. The pain was too much and he passed out with the scent of his burning flesh attacking his nose.

Chapter 3

He could hear her singing as he was coming back around. She shoved some pills down his throat and made him drink something that smelled like urine to wash it down. He gagged but managed to get the pill down. "Good boy, your new home is ready for you." she said, dragging him back to the hole by his hurt shoulder. With all his might he kicked her square in the chest, knocking the air out of her. Even in extreme amounts of pain he jumped up and ran to the other side of the basement towards the stairs.

Then he felt a painful tugging in his back and he collapsed screaming. Doing his best to bend his arm backward he realized he had a meat hook in his back that was attached to the wall. Hot blood started to ooze down his back. "Did you really think I was stupid enough to leave an exit for you?" Katie laughed and jerked the heavy cable line attached to his hook making him fall backwards.

After a few minutes of dragging and pulling him she was able to toss him in the hole. The grate sliced up his legs like he was made of butter. "Enjoy your new home darling. I would love to stay and chat but I have to get ready for a date tonight." His head swarmed, *A date? How could she be going on a date?* he wondered silently to himself.

"Oh don't worry I am not going to fuck him or anything. He has aids. I just need to lure him home with me. Then the real fun will begin." She said with a twisted smile on her face then slammed the door shut. Once again he was plunged into darkness.

He could feel the grate slowly grating against his bones as he tried to sit. At this point he didn't care. The pill she gave him was kicking in and the hole was spinning around with such a speed it was making him nauseous.

He closed his eyes and let sleep take over. He would rather see Mellie die then have to deal with the pain. He slept hard and surprisingly long. When he woke up, the great had eventually hit bone and had scabbed up around it.

Chapter 4

"Oh good you are awake!" Katie exclaimed with joy. "This is Harvey." With that she shoved the man into the hole with him. Mitch noticed he was also naked and severely bruised. "This is what happens to dogs when they cheat on their wives." She slammed the door, leaving them both in the dark. The man was sobbing and Mitch was pinned on the grate with nowhere to move.

Katie opened the door again and heaved him up. She put a matching hook and cable in his back like Mitch's. Then dragged Mitch up. "There both dogs are chained up." she said with a determined voice.

"Mitch, you are going to want to turn around and face the wall."She said quietly. " No." Mitch said looking at her in the eyes. "Suit yourself." She kicked him in the jaw making him drop to the floor. His jaw started to swell and throb. She yanked his mouth open and put a dental vice in to make sure his mouth remained open.

Then she pushed the man to face Mitch. "Suck his cock." Mitch shook his head no. Katie fisted his head pushing his face against the man's flaccid cock. "Suck him NOW!" suddenly the man's cock grew in his mouth gagging him. It stuck really bad and was a tinted green color.

Katie pushed him to where he was on his hands and knees. "Fuck him." Katie demanded the man.
Without a warning the man started to ram Mitch hard in the ass. Screaming Mitch tried to move away. "See this is why you shouldn't cheat. Make sure you tear him up." she yelled to the man, who was grunting heavily and pounding him like an angry lover. Mitch started to scream and sob." This is what happens to my heart when you decide to cheat. You feel my pain." The man was thrusting harder and harder grunting like a wild

animal. Harvey came hard and Mitch could feel blood running down his leg as he pulled out.

"You bitch." Mitch sobbed and Katie laughed. "Oh by the way Harvey here has more than just aids. " With that being said she pulled a gun and shot him in the head. His brains and blood splattering all over Mitch's back."One more thing sweetie, I'm not going to feed you anymore. You will have to just consume Harvey here. " She shoved both men in the hole and closed the lid over the cables that were still attached also.

Chapter 5

Every part of Mitch hurt and ached. The grate slicing deeper and deeper into his thighs. The stench of Harvey was making him want to throw up. *I should have done some sort of background check on that bitch before I married her.* Mitch thought silently. Harvey sat up and Mitch screamed. Harvey laughed, "Relax man,

I'm just in your mind. I'm still very much dead. Sorry about the ramming. It had been so long since I had sex."

Mitch shuddered but was happy to have someone talk to him in the hole. "What all did you have disease wise?" Mitch whispered. "I lost track to be honest. You see I was a lonely man and I favored male prostitutes. I found one I fell in love with. Ricky and I shared needles filled with heroin and fucked around the clock. Ricky died, and at his funeral I found out he was basically a petri dish full of diseases." Harvey said sadly. "What's the deal with your crazy wife?" Harvey asked.

"I messed up and was caught cheating. I didn't realize that she was 7 sides of crazy." Mitch said, pushing Harvey's dead body to where he was on the grate and Mitch wasn't. "Sorry man but I can't take that grate anymore." Mitch whispered to Harvey. "No problem, it's not like I can feel it." Harvey said laughing.

"I got to escape her, Harvey you have to help me." Mitch whispered. "Ok but you are going to need your strength. That bitch is crazy strong. Take a few bites out of my leg and let's get some sleep." Harvey said in a soothing voice. "Yea, it's not like I am already fucked with a ticking time bomb."Mitch laughed then picked up the lifeless leg and ripped through the sturdy muscle with his teeth. The bite was salty at first but Mitch closed his eyes thinking of steak. Before he realized it he had several huge bites. Feeling full for the first time in weeks he slept on top of Harvey's body.

Chapter 6
He could hear sawing. For a moment Mitch forgot where he was, but then a blinding pain erupted at his ankles and it all came screaming back. He opened his eyes just long enough to see his wife

sawing off his foot with a power saw. He watched her rip at the tendons until it was free. Then came the blowtorch. Mitch screamed and started to thrash around. He tried to push her away but realized he didn't have hands anymore. "There, now this is just in case you were planning on some sort of escape. " His wife laughed maniacally. "Why are you doing this? I know I messed up but you could have just divorced me." Mitch wailed. "No I couldn't. I don't believe in divorce. You made your mistake and you have to pay the price. That's it." She said firmly.

She kicked him hard in the ribs and he could feel them snapping. "Is that all you got?" He muttered, spitting out blood. She laughed then shoved him back in the hole. Harvey was gone except a couple of body parts. "I left you some dinner but I can't have you getting comfortable. Your place is on that grate." She said slamming down the lid. He could hear her singing and moving something heavy over the lid.

He could feel the lid bend with the pressure and it started to smash into his head. Sighing in pain and frustration Mitch did his best to scoot away from the lid. Harvey appeared again. "Hey man, you aren't looking too good." Harvey said. Mitch sobbed quietly, his chest heaving. He could hear his wife building something above the hole. "You are going to die here, she's rebuilding the basement where this isn't a part of it anymore. "Harvey whispered. "I know man, I know." Mitch said miserably.

"I just want all this torture to end. I have paid for my crime. I just want to die." "Well there is a way, but it's going to be tricky. You may have to eat some more of me to get access. You can run your throat against that grate." Harvey whispered. Mitch realized he was right. But in his way was Harvey's head and arm. "Well at least I'll die full."Mitch said, wincing in pain.

He started to tear at the flesh with his teeth doing his best to consume almost everything. He felt full and finally had made enough room to lay down enough where his throat was resting on the grate. "Here's to nothing." He whispered to Harvey. He started to saw his throat using the grate. He could smell his blood that was rushing out of his neck like a hot river. Harvey smiled in approval. Everything went black for Mitch, but his hatred and anger made him linger around.

Chapter 7

Mitch felt like an astronaut must feel in space, weightless. He floated up from his hole and watched in fascination as his wife built a new basement. *She is so handy. I never realized she was capable of building anything.* He thought to himself. He tried to wrench the hammer out of her hand but his hand just slipped through. *Ugh even in death, she's hard to take out.*Mitch thought. As on cue Harvey appeared beside him. "You need some souls to make you stronger." He whispered to Mitch motioning outside.

Mitch appeared outside watching everyone else rush around him and some through him. *"How exactly am I supposed to get stronger?"* Mitch asked Harvey who appeared beside him. "Wait until someone gets killed. Then take over the killer's body and eat his brain from within." Harvey said.

Should be easy enough, after all it was New York. Mitch thought to himself as he began to float towards a dark alley. There was a man raping a woman in one of the alley's and stepped into his body. His brain was easy to find and took a huge bite of it. The taste was vile and sour. Shuddering he slammed out of the body and landed on the ground behind him.

The man continued to grunt unaware of anything else.

"Not that one, that's already a ghost. You can tell because of the darkness that surrounds him." Harvey said laughing. "Fucker." Mitch said dry heaving. "Hey I have to have some fun, considering my end." Harvey said with his eyes gleaming. "Enough with wasting time. In case you have forgotten my wife is still out there and still pissed off." Mitch said angrily. "Fine fine, this way. There is a man that is holding a bank hostage. Eat his brain." Harvey said, sighing. Quickly they both floated into the bank. Once again Mitch went into the gun man's body. This time the brain tasted sweet almost like honey. The man flung himself on the ground screaming while bleeding from the eyes. Mitch couldn't stop, the taste was so intoxicating. Immediately Mitch felt stronger, but one brain wasn't going to be enough to take down the bitch he married.

Chapter 8

Mitch never felt so alive, eating the brains of the bad guys was better than any other drug he had ever tried. Soon he was walking around with the living picking up objects and hurling them. It was such a rush. But there would be plenty of time for enjoyment right now he had to go back to his wife. Even in death, she was still irritating him.

He made his way back to his house and passed right through the front door. "Honey! I'm home."Mitch screamed. His wife came around the corner into the living room and screamed. "How did you get out?" She demanded. "Oh, I died!"Mitch said laughing and threw her into the kitchen. "I'm going to repay you for everything you have ever done. You will beg for death when I am done with you." Mitch screamed, wrapping the phone cord around her neck.

Instead she started to laugh. Mitch confused asked her why she was laughing. "Because I have this!" She produced a small vial. "What is that?" Mitch asked once again, feeling fear. "Oh this? This is your new prison!" She screamed then uncorked the vile. A strong wind started to suck Mitch into the vile. "NNOOOOO!" Mitch screamed feeling every part of his metaphysical body being crammed into the vial. She put the cork back on and hung it around her neck. "See it pays to be prepared for little bastards like yourself breaking my heart." With that she put one drop of acid in the vial and listened to the tiny screams. She smiled and went about cooking dinner.

Chapter 9

Katie's good mood didn't last long when her front door suddenly shattered from the force of a shotgun. Splinters of wood flew everywhere, and Katie had just enough time to duck. Even though he was in great pain, Mitch stopped screaming and watched closely out of his vial. Three huge men came barrelling into the house like they were linemen for a football team.

"Boss wants to see you!" One of them angrily snapped. Mitch was confused, boss? What the hell were they talking about? As far as he knew his wife never got into any sort of trouble. She was the very definition of a stepford wife. They roughly grabbed her and dragged her out of the house. Mitch was glad she was being handled so roughly. She kept her head down as they drove her to what looked like a giant casino on the edge of town.

She allowed herself to be taken to the top floor. There was a big man in an expensive pinstripe suit with gold rings on every finger sitting at a big oak desk. "Miss Katie. Where have you been?" The man spoke quietly. "My husband cheated on me, so I was teaching him a lesson. I guess time just slipped away." Katie said miserably.

"It's been almost a year. That's a bit more than just slipping away from someone. I get the impression you don't want to pay off your gambling debts!" His voice boomed and Mitch could feel the vibrations in his vial. He could see tears rolling up in her eyes. "I will pay you back, I promise." She was sobbing. "Too little, too late, Miss Katie."

The men grabbed Katie by the arms and cut off her wrist with one swift cut with an extremely sharp sword. She barely winced. "I have something you want. I could give it to you, and clear my debt!" She screamed hugging her wrist to her now soaked shirt.

"What is it that you have that I could possibly want other than my money?" The man in the chair said as he loudly popped his knuckles. "I have a daughter named Matilda. She's fourteen and is living at a private school in Gully's Lurch, about an hour from here. You can have her and do what you want with her." Katie said breathing hard. Mitch couldn't believe what he was hearing. His perfect wife had a gambling problem and she was willing to sell Matilda to settle her debt? What sort of deranged piece of shit person would do that? Mitch screamed his rage and beat his tiny fist against the vial.

The man watched Katie who had started to shiver from blood loss. "Fine, bring her here." He snapped his fingers and the men dipped her wrist into liquid nitrogen. It immediately stopped bleeding and turned like a crystal ash color. Chunks of her skin sparkled in the light as her entire stump crystalized.

Katie nodded and ran out of the casino. She lifted a quarter from one of the older men's winnings when he wasn't paying attention. She was able to find a lobby phone much like an old pay phone. "Matilda? I need you to come home immediately. Have your cousin bring you to the Spoiled Larks Casino. Please hurry."

Chapter 10

She sank down on the curb and started to sob. She could feel the vial pulsate with all of Mitch's tiny fists beating against the glass. "I fucked up Mitch. I started gambling while you rotted away in your hole. I felt so empty and betrayed, so full of pain, it was the only thing that made me feel better. I started off winning so I was able to make the renovations to the basement. Then I started to lose, I sold my body, I started to get addicted to drugs. I sold all of your things, I did everything I could to break even. Eventually, I realized I couldn't stop. No matter how much I tortured you, I could not stop going to the casino. The only thing I have left is Matilda. Once I give her up for good, and pray she doesn't end up in some sort of sex ring, I'll be able to walk away. I will be able to just focus on the cocaine addiction I seem to be battling." She whispered holding onto the vial.

Mitch didn't care to hear her sob story, and there was no way he was going to let Matilda be thrown into a bad situation like that. The pain from the acid was really making his body throb but he couldn't let it consume him. He was going to have to find a way to save his daughter from his crazy wife. He may be stuck in the vial, but come hell or high water he was going to do everything he could think of to try and save her. He may have been a shitty husband to Katie, and maybe it was a little bit his fault she went off the deep end, but he had paid for his sins. There was no reason why his daughter should suffer as well. Time lost all meaning inside the vial and the next thing he knew, he could see Matilda being dragged out of a black van. They picked up Katie who was still sobbing on the curb and brought them both back upstairs.

Matilda looked scared as she cowered against the big men that held her up by her arms. "Mom, what is going on? Where is dad?" She whispered.

The shuddering of Katie's breath started to shake the vial. Mitch tried to pound on the vial to get Matilda's attention. He wanted her to run whenever she got the chance, but sadly, all he could do was sit there and watch.

Katie started to sob loudly as the men tied Matilda to a post. The ropes were laced with razor blades and small trails of blood decorated her body. The more she struggled the deeper the razor blades bit into her flesh, like an angry dog ripping at a steak. "What are you going to do?" Katie sobbed.

"We are going to take your debts out in flesh." The man said cracking his knuckles loudly. Katie stood up and said," Go ahead and take what you want from my body." The man laughed so hard it looked like his pinstripes were dancing. "That's funny, Miss Katie. I didn't say whose body I was going to take my payment from." He nodded and the guys all smiled. "NOOOO DON'T YOU TOUCH HER!" Katie screamed but was rewarded with a giant veiny fist in the nose. Mitch couldn't see which one threw the punch but silently was cheering the guys one. Katie deserved everything she got, Matilda did not.

"You owe 50,000 so I think your beautiful daughter will be whipped that many times. It's going to take a little bit, but the nice thing is the belts my guys are going to use are laced with all sorts of sharp things embedded in it." The man laughed again. Matilda started to scream. The belts looked as thick as sponges used for washing cars. The air felt electric as the belts whipped through the air. There was so much noise going on, it was hard to focus on what was going on.

Stringy, bloodied pieces of flesh were flying in every direction as the belts ripped Matilda apart. Mitch was screaming and doing everything he could think of to get out of the vial, and to save his daughter. Eventually, everything went silent except for Katie's sobs. There was hardly anything recognizable on Matilda. She was a blobby bloody mess against the pole. The men grabbed Katie and brought her face to face with the man in the pinstripe suit. "That's an interesting necklace Miss Katie, I am going to need that as well." The man said, holding out his massive hand. "I don't think you want this." Katie began to protest. Her hand went protectively around the vial. The man grabbed her hand and snapped every bone in it loudly. He ripped the necklace off of her neck and peered closely at it. Mitch started to beat the vial with his fists hoping the big man would see him. "Get her the fuck out of my sight. If you ever set foot in ANY casino again even if it's just to take a piss, I will sell you to the worst sort of monsters you can imagine." The men nodded and dragged Katie away.

Chapter 11

The man was sitting there in the silence looking at the vial very closely. Mitch did everything he could think of to break the glass and get some sort of attention from the man. "Well isn't this interesting?" He whispered then slammed the vial down on the desk as hard as he could. The acid that was Mitch's tomb splashed all over the desk causing a small hole. Mitch sat up sputtering and looked at the man. "Let me guess, you're the husband huh? She did a number on you." The man leaned down and whispered to Mitch.

Mitch nodded the cold air hurting his body. There was still acid in his lungs. It took him a minute to get the strength to talk and when he did it only came out as a whisper. "I never thought I would be free from that hell she put me in. I want revenge for my daughter." The man nodded and cracked his knuckles which caused Mitch to scream from the sound echoing in his small damaged ears.

"Luckily for you, I am not an ordinary business man. Now, I can't really undo what she has already done except make you tall again. You make a deal with me that I can't refuse, and I will give you your revenge. Katie had mentioned that you cheated on her. Infidelity is not something I tolerate. I will grant you a deal however, I think you should still be punished for what you have done." The man quietly said. Mitch slowly stood up and whispered, "Whatever the price I shall pay it." Mitch smiled and the man whispered something to Mitch that he couldn't understand.

Mitch felt like he was being put through a shredder as his bones painfully popped loudly through his skin. He was getting taller albeit slowly. It took a good hour before he was bigger than before. "Alright Mitch, my name is Mr. Rumple. Let's hear your deal." He said cracking his knuckles. "Whatever you need Mr. Rumple. I just want people to hurt. Matilda was innocent and didn't deserve her fate." Mitch said in between small gasps. It still hurt to breathe.

Mr. Rumple snorted. "Innocent? Your precious daughter is far from innocent. No one ends up in my office that is innocent. I don't hurt innocent people." Mitch felt confused. He stood there for a moment trying not to break down and cry. "Your daughter has her own rap sheet. Everything to breaking and entering, fraud, drug trafficking and aggravated assault. I have her file right here. Take a look." He said pushing the file to Mitch. Mitch felt like his entire world was collapsing on him. He had been so focused on his affair, he missed everything vital in his life.

Mitch looked at the file feeling sick to his stomach. She had done some despicable things and he felt rageful. Without thinking about it, he punched Mr. Rumple right in the nose as hard as he could. Blood spewed out of his nose and his nose looked horribly crooked. Mr. Rumple smiled and cracked his nose back into place with his big fingers. He wiped the blood off with his silk handkerchief. "Hilarious, that will cost you." At that moment, Mitch realized that he had fucked up.

For a brief moment he started to miss his vial that hung around his incredibly selfish wife. Mr. Rumple grabbed him up by the neck and slammed him into the ground. "You will get your revenge but you will never have your freedom." Mr. Rumple snarled. "I have the special place just for you." Mr. Rumple started to punch Mitch into the face and each ring left a special imprint. Teeth, blood and some small scraps of skin went flying. Mitch was gagging on his own blood but didn't try to fight him off. Mitch knew he was overpowered. Mr. Rumple dragged him to a closet. "See this is a prison cell that only a special key can open, you will be trapped in this prison for all eternity. You will be able to get your revenge on your 'meals' that will be dropped off to you. Once you hit 20 'meals' you will be on to your next punishment." Mr. Rumple whispered into Mitch's ear.

The cell was no bigger than Mitch's body and was filled with steel that bent inwards. There was a small, dirty, stained mattress. Nothing more, nothing less. Mitch started to try and back pedal but Mr. Rumple shoved him in then shut the door. Mitch was plunged into a darkness that felt like it was a heavy weighted blanket. It felt like Mitch's breath was caught in his throat. He had never experienced such pressing darkness and for the first time in his life, he was afraid. There was never any light, no food and no sort of entertainment. Time lost all sort of meaning, he spent the time regretting hitting Mr. Rumple. Eventually the door opened after what felt like years being in the darkness that never seemed to get any better. "Your wife has been taken care of, her sister set her on fire. However, you don't get to even see her because of punching me. She gets her own place on my farm. You will get your first meal in a few days." Mr. Rumple said as he spit into Mitch's face. "Feel free to do whatever you wish to your meal, it will stay alive until you get another meal."

"I am not going to do anything to them!" Mitch screamed as one last surge of rage flowed through him. "Oh I have heard that before, the longer you are kept in there, the longer you find yourself doing all sorts of despicable acts to ease your pain." Mr. Rumple laughed hard until his face turned red. "Fine, punish me, but just know that one day I will be getting free." Mitch said sadly. Mr. Rumple locked the prison door and pocketed the key. The key is the one I use to throw Mitch his food. However, he is no longer trying to get out, in fact he actually has taken a liking to being in there. Mr. Rumple was right, Mitch has done some pretty despicable things to his meals. He hasn't regretted anything he has done.

Part 4

I looked over to see if Jason was listening to my story. He was muttering to himself and drooling blood everywhere. "It's been an hour, let's see if I can take you to Mitch." I said admiring my handiwork. I called Lollie, but to my dismay, it was going to be a little bit longer. "Sorry doll, I know you need to get to that prison, but we found some things in the house that deserve extra." Lollie said angrily. She filled me in and my jaw dropped. "What the actual fuck?" I said with my breath catching in my throat. "You kept souvenirs of all your kills? You kept a body part from each person? The most you kept was from my cousin!" I was screaming, and I couldn't stop.

I was kicking him as hard as I could until I could no longer feel my foot. "What in the fuck is wrong with you?" I was breathing hard and he was barely making a sound. I had to stop so I didn't kill him, I needed him to go to Mitch. "What was so special about Claira?" I whispered as I sank to the floor. His eyes were rolling back into his head and drool with blood slid down his chin. "Oh no, you don't get to die." I said getting angrier. I went to the table and started to dig around in the suitcase I had brought with me. It was loaded to the brim with everything I could possibly need for any situation.

It took me a couple of minutes to find what I was looking for, a huge syringe filled with strong powerful concoctions I had made. I stabbed it right into his chest and watched as the greenish, purplish, thick, sludge went into his chest. I watched as his muscles began to extend like a hard bodybuilder's pecs. Smiling, I watched as all of his veins slowly turned black and began to protrude through the skin. His mouth jerked open and his tongue flopped out. I waited until his body stopped jerking. "There, isn't that better?" I said trying to take a deep breath.

He looked alert enough so I slapped him as hard as I could. "Now answer my fucking question! What was so special about Claira?" My heart was knocking loud against my chest. "I took her because she reminded me of you! I never got over you, so I took her. I kept her for five years! She was my favorite and once she died, I couldn't part with just one souvenir." He sobbed. "She didn't deserve that or anything that you did to her. You can bet, I would sign another deal just to make sure you continue to live and suffer. I would do anything to make sure you felt everything you put each victim through!" I screamed.

I lit another cigarette and sat there watching him as I was trying to keep from shaking. Out of everyone I had tortured this one was the most emotional one. I hated to feel anything. The acrid smoke filled my lungs from my menthol cigarette and slowly I began to calm down. It was time to do a couple more tortures that I wouldn't normally do. He was my last one and it deserved a much better thought out torture.

I lit another cigarette, it was weird I was chain smoking, that was something I had never done. What I was about to do was going to take a lot of powering through. I let the smoke from the cigarette burn my lungs before I blew it out. "Well Jason, this next stage of my torture is going above anything I have ever done, not that I need to explain myself to you. This is going to be for Claira however, so you know it's going to be bad for you." I smiled.

I couldn't find the tools I needed on the table, so thinking he wouldn't be stupid enough to run away, I left him to go find what I needed in the other room. I was throwing tools against the wall as fast as I could grab them. I stopped because I heard a loud noise coming from Jason's room. Grabbing a chisel I ran back to

Jason. He had somehow managed to flip himself over on his face. "God damn it! You are such a pain in the ass but luckily for you, you just saved me a step." I laughed. He was spitting blood and maggots on the floor. He was making a horrible gurgling sound that sounded like a backed up sink drain.

I grabbed the rubber mallet and sat on his legs right on his broken knee caps. I took the chisel and took a deep breath, then rammed it as hard as I could right into his asshole. I swung the mallet hard on the end of the chisel until just a small tip of it was sticking out. I slowly pulled it out holding my breath. I had just enough grip on the tip of the handle that didn't end up in his ass. I flipped him over and shoved the chisel into his mouth. He was gagging and shuddering as I kept ramming the chisel harder and harder into the back of his mouth. I was about to do it one more time when my phone rang. "Hey doll, I am stopping by the jail. Meet me in about

20 minutes." Lollie said hurriedly then hung up the phone.

"Luckily for you, it's time to go." I said as I spit in his face. I used his tongue to clean off the chisel then picked him up. Surprisingly, the wheels on his feet made it easy for me to wheel him into the van I had parked in the garage. I chained his arm to the bottom of my seat then climbed into the driver seat and began to drive. My head felt muddled with rage and emotions. I could hear him sliding about in the back of the van as I drove.

I lit the last cigarette in my pack and crumbled up the box. It was bitter sweet, because I knew that I would have to quit smoking for good. I made sure I hit all the potholes on the way to the jail Lollie and I had both agreed upon. I got to the prison and Lollie was there waiting for me. She was rapidly chewing gum like when she was pissed off. "Sorry about the delay." She said as she popped in another piece of gum. "What's wrong Lollie?" I asked as we hurriedly wheeled Jason into an empty jail cell. "I found the body of my little sister who just disappeared a few days ago. She was 9 and was found under his bed." Lollie said, holding back some tears.

She kicked him hard enough to see the rib poke out of his mutilated flesh. I could feel her rage and for the first time I felt scared of her. She grabbed a hold of his hair and started to rip out the hair by the root. Blood was coming out of his scalp like a small waterfall. I slowly produced the key from around my neck and put my hand on Lollie. "Let Mitch take care of the rest of him." I whispered. I wanted to keep torturing him, but I knew once I got him in the cell with Mitch it would get ten times worse. Lollie took a deep breath and nodded. I unlocked the cell and saw Mitch chewing on a finger in the dark. I wheeled Jason onto the dirty mattress. Mitch stood up and smiled. "My last meal?" He whispered. He looked sad as he eyed Jason up and down. "You did a number on this one." He pouted.

"I didn't do enough. This is Jason, he is a pedophile who killed Claira and many others, including Lollie's little sister." I said as Mitch stuck his finger into Jason's scalp and licked off some blood. "Enjoy your last meal Mitch. Nice knowing you." I said as I backed away from the cell. I could hear him whisper to Jason "I wish she didn't do such a number on you, I would have loved to have more fun with you". I locked it back and gave Lollie a hug.

"Don't worry, Mitch will make him suffer. I am so sorry for your loss." I whispered to her. She sniffled for a second then straightened up her police badge on her uniform. "I'm going to miss you. I am going to go on that Bahama's vacation now, thanks to you." We parted ways and jumped back into the van. I drove it to a small lake and stripped off my skimpy police costume and threw it in the van. I put a brick on the gas pedal and let it slide into the lake.

I quickly changed into my normal clothes and walked the five blocks to where I had hidden my car. I climbed in my car and locked the doors. I started the car and let the ac run on full blast until I had goosebumps. My breath was coming in shudders and tears were sliding down my face. I quickly wiped the tears away and carefully applied a small amount of makeup. I threw my car into gear and blasted some music enough to send vibrations through my muscles. I had one more task before I was going to meet Mortimer and my daughter for my early retirement.

I began to drive towards the destination I had tattooed on my arm. The day I made my deal the man had given me an address. "You better figure out some way not to lose this address, because if you do lose it there will be hell to pay. You have 12 hours to deliver the key back to me after you deliver your last revenge to Mitch. If you fail to be there, I will turn you into a vitamin for pregnant women!" He had said as he pushed a tiny piece of paper in my hand. I had clutched it into my fist for hours as I walked home to get into some dry clean clothes. By the time I got home the piece of paper had started to dig into my palm. The writing almost wasn't legible. I turned it into a tattoo so I would never lose it. It was written in another language so no one would figure it out where I was going. It was written inside of a rose I had hidden on my arm so that way no one would notice that I had a tattoo in the workforce. As I drove I thought about each and every one of my conquests in the name of revenge. I should have felt relieved that it was all over with, instead I felt like I wasn't going to belong. All these years I had always kept the fact that I was a bounty hunter for a mysterious man from my normal life. It felt weird that I wouldn't be doing it anymore.

Part 5

The drive to the location was starting to get bumpy and the trees were becoming gnarled. The trees looked like they were part of a spook house all decorated on Halloween. Giant pothole after pothole scraped the bottom of my car making me grip the wheel with both hands and grit my teeth together. I had never taken the time to actually go to this location before, I always tried to follow the instructions completely.

I was starting to get nervous and sweat started to pour down my back in a sticky river. I turned on the ac and turned up some music a slight notch. I could feel eyes watching me as darkness began to cover my car like a huge blanket. I no longer felt like a powerful bounty hunter but a small insignificant ant. Branches started to smack the car as I drove further down what looked like to be a long driveway that had been forgotten.

I cranked the ac up as far as it could go and ran over another pothole, this time popping my tire. I slowly got out and looked at the now shredded tire with a piece of rebar sticking into it. I checked my cell phone for the time and realized I was running low on time. I tucked the cell phone in my pocket and started to run for it. With every step I took I felt like my entire body had been dipped into terrifyingly cold cement.

My hair hung damply around my shoulders like a wet paper bag and my breath was coming out in short shudders. Every muscle in my body hurt so bad and I knew I wasn't in bad shape. Finally after what seemed like an eternity I made it to a huge house that looked like it didn't belong there. The outside of the house looked shabby in a spooky sort of way.

The paint was a dark color and the door handle felt sticky like it was covered in blood.

I walked in and felt a wave of nausea hit me like a bag of cement. The inside was beautifully decorated in golds and reds. It was dazzling and overwhelming but I couldn't focus on it. I kept walking to the main room to see the man standing in front of a shelf. "Abby! You made it with thirty seconds to spare! I am impressed." He said quietly. For the first time I was able to actually see his face and was surprised. He had the darkest green eyes I had ever seen and every time I looked into them I felt nauseous again. I pulled the necklace from my neck breaking the silver chain I had always kept it on. The chain seemed to disappear like it was never in my hand. The key felt heavy and warm in my palm as I handed it to the man.

"You look pale Abby, you should sit down and drink some water." He motioned to the chair by a desk that looked like it was a throne. Something didn't feel right and I knew I should have ran out of the room, but instead I found myself sitting down. He offered me a nice cool glass of water that was the best tasting water I had ever had. "This place has a tendency of making people dizzy." He laughed.

My tongue felt like it had a coating of spray paint on it and my limbs felt like they were heavy. "I never properly introduced myself, my name is Mr. Rumple. I don't really remember my first name, it's been many years since anyone has called me it. Think of me like a modern day Rumplestiltskin from your fairy tales you used to read as a child. As you know, I make deals with people for a price. I must say that in all the years that I have done this, you are the first one to take me by surprise. Not only were your revenge quests, creative, they were far from boring. I was surprised to see how much your last quest got to you, here all this time I thought you didn't have a heart." He quietly said as he sat down in front of me.

"Why do I feel so funny?" I said trying to keep the room from spinning around. "Well on your last quest you said you would do anything to make another deal correct?" He asked. I felt too heavy to question how he knew anything. I simply nodded. I did not like how I was feeling, each second it was getting worse. "So my dear Abby, would you like to make another deal with me?" He said as he clapped his hands loudly together. I shook my head no, all I wanted was to go home and be done with everything. I took another drink from the water and couldn't keep my body from crumpling to the floor. I could no longer keep my eyes open and the carpet was so soft it lured me to sleep. I felt Mr. Rumple picked me up like I weighed nothing. Cradled up next to his chest, I could briefly smell a horrible smell that reminded me of a rotting corpse. "The water was drugged my pet, once you wake up, we will talk more about doing another deal with me." I heard him whisper in my ear. His lips brushed my ear and then my forehead, however both were not gentle. It was almost like he smashed his mouth on a lit stove top then firmly pressed them on my face.

I tried to struggle and wake up but my eyes felt like they were being weighed down with concrete. I felt him put on a bed that oddly felt squishy like it was a water bed. I lay there unable to slip into a deep sleep and unable to move. I was alone with my thoughts as whatever drugs that were in the water, ran rapidly through my body. I felt like I was a child again after my mother had hit me hard enough to the floor. Eventually I lay there long enough for the drugs to wear out of my system. When I opened my eyes, I was surprised to see myself in a brightly lit up room. Looking around made me gasp, and made me miss the drugs. This room looked like it was completely made of humans. The bed I was laying on was decorated with bones and what I thought was water was actually blood.

I tried to backpedal off the bed and fell hard on my elbow. Unpleasant pain jolted through my body but I ignored it as I pushed myself off of the floor. I threw open the door and ran down the stairs as fast as my still rubber–like legs could carry me. I ran out of the house and was halfway back to the highway before I allowed myself to stop and catch my breath.

I knew my car was still there with a flat tire but there was no way I was going to go back for it. I calmed myself down and called myself a taxi. I knew I was going to have to walk to the nearest town but at least then I could get another car from a dealer with the help of the taxi. Luckily for me the nearest town wasn't too far away.

By the time I made it into town I was starting to slowly feel better again. Within an hour I was sitting in a brand new car. I had never kept anything personal in any of my cars, just in case I had to ditch them. Everything I needed was on my phone or under the case of it. Once more I was on my way to Mortimer and my retirement.

I felt uneasy as I drove, something just didn't feel right. I felt too hot and had cranked up the ac as far as it would go. By the time I got to the cabins by the lake where Mortimer and I first met, my hands were practically slipping off the steering wheel. I walked in and couldn't shake the feeling that darkness was trying to smother me. I felt around for the light switch and turned it on. Mortimer was sitting in the dark and it looked like he had been crying. "Hi babe, what's wrong?" I was afraid of the answer. I had never seen him look like this before and I didn't know how to react to it. "Where's Abileen?"

I went over to him and sat down in front of him. Mortimer wiped a tear from his eyes and sighed loudly. He opened his mouth but no sound came out. I heard clapping behind me and whirled around face to face with Mr. Rumple. "Mortimer, what is he doing here? What in the fuck is going on?" I said, starting to feel angry. "Well you ran away before I was able to talk to you." Mr. Rumple said, helping himself to a chair. "Um, Abby?" Mortimer finally spoke. I faced him trying not to let my anger show. "I've known the entire time what you have been doing. I got curious about your scars and I met Mr. Rumple one night who said he would tell me as long as I made a deal with him."

I felt my knees knock together and I sank to the floor. "What did you promise?" I whispered suddenly my breath caught in my throat. Mortimer started to sob quietly, taking me by surprise, because I had never seen him cry. I took his hands in mine and asked again, "What did you promise? Where is Aibleen?"

"She is at your grandmothers, I uh, didn't bring her. She is safe and not part of my deal. I made the deal with Mr. Rumple here that after your last revenge, you would continue to work for him as his own personal bounty hunter. My price will be that he has my soul instead of yours, so you can be here for Aibleen. She needs her mother not so much me." Mortimer said as he wiped away a tear. He put my hands close to his chest. "I know it sounds bad babe, but I did it so that way you can have the rest of your life with our daughter." He whispered as he brushed a dark red strand of hair out of my face.

"I was done! I had done my last one, I was going to retire!" I sobbed. Mr. Rumple cleared his throat, "Yes, that's true. However, you wouldn't have that dream retirement you so wanted. After you would have returned the key, I was going to claim your soul and grind your body into my newest batch of vitamins. Without Mortimer's deal, I had no use for you. You saw the room you were going to die in, I was preparing your body for the vitamins I feed to the dumb pregnant women who made deals with me."

"When are you going to takc Mortimer?" I whispered, choking back the tears. I didn't have time to cry right now, I had to be strong. "He will remain with you unless you try to get out of his contract. If you do anything that irritates me, anything at all, even if it's a new perfume, I will take him. I will make him suffer greatly already more than he is going to." Mr. Rumple stood up and straightened his cufflinks. "What do you say Abby?" He said flashing a dazzling white smile. "Keep in mind if you refuse, you will be bringing Aibleen into this as well." He laughed and straightened his tie. "Fine, you have a deal." I sighed and stood up. "What happens now?" I said in a strong voice, I felt defeated but didn't want to show him that. "Mitch is no longer in the cell, however he was replaced with Jason. You have to feed everyone on my list to Jason now. If you don't Mitch is going to torture you. I decided to make Mitch my key enforcer with those who try to break out of their contracts with me. Everyone you will kill, is a very bad person who not only has gone back on their deals with me, but makes Jason look like a saint." Mr. Rumple handed me back the key I had worn around my neck for twenty years. Wrapped around the key was a thick piece of paper that has names neatly written.

"Why can't Jason starve?" I said as he began to move closer to the front door. "Just because your dear sweet Mortimer gave his soul to me doesn't mean that your life is going to be free from pain and strife. Jason will be fed like Mitch was, end of story." He said firmly as he opened the door. "Mortimer enjoy your hell." He laughed then was gone.

I couldn't breathe. I was stuck having to deal with Jason some more in order to protect my daughter. Mortimer began to cough and his face turned an ashy gray. I helped him lay down on the couch. He started to shake and cough up blood. He was coughing up enough blood that I was starting to become concerned. I helped him into my car and started to speed off to the next town. He didn't notice the new car and the drive was quiet. I kept thinking about everything and he was trying not to cough up blood all over the inside of his shirt.

Part 6

We were still in the hospital by the next morning. The doctor had every test known to man run on Mortimer, but there wasn't much they could figure out. I was feeling more than defeated and I couldn't look Mortimer in the face. I excused myself and went for a drive to go get Aibleen. I watched my grandma help Aibleen with her homework and realized I was going to have to do some things first before I could take her home with me.

I quietly snuck back to my car and floor it back to Mr. Rumple's place. I didn't bother to knock, just walked right in. He must have been waiting for me because he was sitting down sipping on a martini that looked like it had an eyeball floating in it. "Ah, Abby back so soon?" He flashed a smile and sucked down his drink including the eyeball. "Why was it so important for me to be your bounty hunter to the point where you had to trick Mortimer in giving up his soul?" I said crossing my arms over my chest.

"Are you fishing around for a compliment?" He said as he poured another martini and plucked a milky white eyeball into it. A thin line of pus from the eyeball floated to the top looking like snot. "No, I want the truth." I muttered not looking away from the glass as the eyeball bounced around in the glass. "Ok, the truth is, I am fascinated by your rage. For the past 20 years you have been my best contract. You got rid of Jason who I admit needed to suffer. If you check your list, you will find his entire family down to his distant cousins are on that list. He is going to have to eat his ENTIRE family." He grinned then licked the eyeball.

I smiled, "Thank you for telling me the truth. Now tell me what is wrong with

Mortimer. This will be the last question so I will be on my way in getting your list completed." I said, finally taking my eyes off of his drink. "Mortimer is suffering from a rare disease that will eventually kill him without a warning. Could be tomorrow, or a 100 years from now. I get to choose when I take his soul. Oh and Abby, I just wanted to let you know that the list will be never ending. Do stop by anytime you want though, I enjoy our visits." He said, showing me to the door. My mind was reeling, neverending? His list was never ending? I was going to be his bounty hunter until he decided it was time to let me die.

I drove back to the hospital and curled next to Mortimer in his hospital bed. "I went back to Mr. Rumple and asked him what was wrong with you. He said it was a rare disease that will kill you at his discretion. The list of bodies I am to kill is never ending." I whispered. I started to sob against his chest. He put his arms around me and held me tight. "It's ok babe, you don't ever have to worry about being a boring housewife, and you get to continue to do what you enjoy to do. Plus since you are going after people bad enough to end up on his list, you are like a superhero." He weakly said, trying not to cough.

"The best part of my life was meeting you. Before I met you, I had a horrible gambling problem, and was addicted to drugs. I was homeless and at one point would do anything for food." He whispered against my neck. I snuggled up closer to him. "Other than the gambling, I had a similar problem. I was addicted to pain, even paid for someone to hurt me." I couldn't believe that after 15 years of being married, this was the first time we actually discussed our past with each other. It felt good to get it all off my chest. "What if I can't keep doing this?" I said, wiping away my tears. "You will keep doing it because that means Aibleen is safe. You will do whatever you can to protect her." He whispered and kissed me.

He was right, and I hated that. I watched him fall asleep then I snuck away. The first person on Mr. Rumple's list was Jason's father. I never got along with Jason's father. He was always a prick, and nothing was ever good enough. When I told him what Jason had done, he just shrugged and said that it didn't sound like something Jason would do. He allowed Jason to destroy all those kid's lives. He did nothing but pretend that Jason was no longer his son. I wasn't sure where he was located and was missing Lollie. As if she was reading my mind, my phone rang. "Hello doll, I am bored with retirement. Please tell me you have a case or project you are working on." She said sounding like it had been awhile since she had slept. I quickly filled her in on the new deal. "I will help you until I die." She breathed. "Lollie, I can't ask you to continue to help me." I began to protest. However, she cut me off, "I don't care what you think. I am helping you and that's final. You don't have to pay me." She said firmly before she hung up the phone on me.

Within twenty minutes I met Lollie at a diner for some breakfast. I told her everything although I did more sobbing than I cared to admit. When I was done with telling her everything she slapped me hard in the face. My cheek was stinging and I could feel it turning bright red. "What the hell was that for?" I was completely shocked she would do such a thing. "Quit your whining. You are cleaning up the streets and you still get to make Jason suffer by forcing him to feed off of his family. That was one thing Mitch always used to complain about was the hunger and the loneliness being stuck in that cell. So quit your bitching, and let's do this." She sipped on her coffee, her eyes shining with a fire I had never seen before. "Are you ok?" I asked her suddenly worried about her mental state.

"I haven't really been eating much or sleeping. I can't deal with my grief therefore I couldn't enjoy the Bahamas. I need a project to help get my mind back to a better place. I don't care if I have to help you until I am on my deathbed, I need to do this." I had never seen lollie so passionate about anything before. It was chilling to say the least. She was the closest thing I had to a friend, so I wiped my tears away and nodded. I was done feeling sorry for myself, it was time I got my ass into gear and went to work. I explained to Lollie that the first person on my list was Jason's dad and that I didn't know where he was. I wrote down the first ten people on the list so that way she could track them all down.

Lollie found Jason's dad in less than ten minutes. I had my mouth full of pie when she exclaimed she found him. I nearly choked on it and did my best to carefully swallow it. Jason's dad, Edgar, was living in a place closer to a city that was about 60 miles away. "Tell you what, I'll go get him and you go visit Mortimer. Then you can go talk to Aibleen and let her know that your job is going to make you travel more, but on the bright side she can stay with your grandma while you are away. Then make sure you tell her you will buy her something each and every time you are away. She's at that age where money is everything." Lollie said quickly, finishing her cheeseburger.

She was already out the door before I could protest, so I paid the bill and did exactly what she said to do. Aibleen was only too happy to stay with my grandma. My grandma was sweet and never knew anything my mom had put me through. She spoiled Aibleen every chance she got and I was happy she was safe. I visited Mortimer but he was asleep and his breathing was shaky. Instead of staying, I went to fix the loft up for more tortures. I had to make sure it was completely escape proof because I couldn't glue everyone to a dolly.

"I am at the loft." I said to Lollie then hung up just like old times. I didn't have my old skimpy cop outfit anymore, but this time I didn't need it. I was dressed in an old t-shirt and jeans with a hole in the knee. I tied my hair back into a ponytail because this time I wasn't luring anyone. I glanced around and decided I didn't really want to keep cleaning it so I put garbage bags down as a walkway.

Lollie showed up at the loft almost an hour later. She must have applied a little bit of makeup because she looked like a beautiful angry doll. Edgar was bleeding from the head and shaking badly as Lollie surprisingly dragged him by his handcuffs. I chained Edgar up with the help of Lollie. We chained him upside down so all of the blood would rush to his head. I lit a cigarette and Lollie grabbed one as well. "I didn't know you smoked." I was shocked. "I am having a hard time getting through all this. My sister is dead, your cousin is dead and now we get to play bounty hunters to feed the monster responsible. Darkness is surrounding my soul and I am desperately trying to keep my head up." She said sadly as she lit the cigarette, took a drag then lit Edgar's head on fire. She watched for a few minutes but the smell of boiling flesh and hair made us both gag. I put the fire out using the Himalayan salt. "I can't do what you do, but it does give me a little bit of light in my shroud of darkness. Whatever you need, you have my help. Don't worry no matter how far I sink into darkness, there is no way I am making a deal for my soul." She managed a small smile and gave me a hug.

I hated the fact that she was in darkness, I knew that feeling all too well. That was the feeling that drove me to my pain addiction. "Hello Edgar, it's been a few years." I said turning my attention to the upside down man. He hasn't aged well over the years. I could see down his shirt to see a giant scar along his chest. "Oh it looks like you have had some work on your heart." I said smiling. He didn't bother to answer and for a minute I thought he died because he was really still. I checked his pulse and found it was really faint. Sighing loudly, I made him fall from his chains then chained him to the floor. His eyes were rolling back in his head and I could see his heart beating literally against his chest.

I sighed in disgust. He was so old and feeble. Anything I had planned for him probably would kill him. I wasn't sure I wanted him to die. I didn't want to do Jason any favors. I slapped him over and over again until he was able to focus on me. "I told you what Jason was doing and you did nothing. As a result he kept doing what he was doing. He eventually hurt so many people. You deserve to feel the pain of everyone he hurt!" I screamed letting the rage course through my body. I grabbed the icepick I used on Jason and poked it right into the iris of his eye, then slowly turned it until the eyeball made a sick popping sound. I left the ruined eyeball still in the socket and moved to break his fingers. "Stop!" Edgar screamed. I shrugged my shoulders and replied, "Now you can see how all those kids felt when they begged Jason to stop."

I hit his fingers one at a time with the sledgehammer until they were all pudgy and purple. Edgar was sobbing but had stopped pleading with me to stop. I took each finger and slowly bent it back until the bone protrude out from his pale, wrinkled flesh. I stood back to admire my handiwork, when I heard my front door to the loft open up. I left Edgar sobbing quietly and went to go investigate. Lollie stood in the main room with an elderly lady with her. "Hi doll, this is his mother.

The rest of his family will be harder to find." She gave his mom a hard push towards me. "Uh, thanks Lollie." I said as I grabbed a hold of Jason's mom and brought her back to where Edgar was. Edgar saw me walk in the room and all of a sudden he came to life. "Miriam!" He yelled as he feebly tried to get the chains off of him. I paid him no attention and got Miriam chained up on the other side of the room.

"Why am I here?" She asked weakly. "You are here because your son Jason turned out to be a pedophile who murdered kids of all ages. When I told Edgar about Jason trying to get to my daughter, he merely shrugged and said nothing. He didn't put a stop to it at all. You are here because you knew what sort of a sick monster he was from a young child, and like your husband, chose to do nothing. You wanted God to fix him, so you sent him to that bible camp where he molested a younger child than himself.

After he got kicked out, you still continued to stick up for him." I said slapping her hard.

I had never tortured two people at the same time. Edgar kept reacting violently to whenever I would slap Miriam, and that gave me an idea. I had read in a story called Twisted Sideways about two people being sewn together as a punishment. I didn't have the needle or the thread so I was going to have to get creative. I continued to hit Miriam as hard as I could until I could hear her bones in her face and ribs start to crack.

I dragged her over to Edgar and threw her down beside him just out of his reach. I took out a syringe that was full of horse tranquilizers and inserted the tip first into Edgar then into Miriam. Soon they were both fast asleep. I pulled out my headphones from my pocket and plugged them into my phone. I dialed Lollie first, "Hey, just wanted to see how you are doing." I said into her voice message machine. I hung up and blasted some music as I began to set to work. It took me a while to cut off all the clothes and to cut through Miriam's back brace. Then I cut them both by the rib cage. I snapped their ribs and started to intermingle their ribs together. I poured the rest of the industrial glue over their ribs and let it harden. I wrapped their old feeble legs together and broke their knees caps with the help of my sledgehammer.

The last thing I did was staple them as much as I could together with an industrial stapler. I called Lollie again this time I got her, relieved I said, "Hey girl the double package is ready. I have the key back to Mitch's cell so I'll need the prison again." Lollie agreed and surprisingly knocked on the loft door within minutes. This time she brought a guard we were friends with. He was giant and extremely toned with muscles. "Hi drew." I said and showed him to the room where Edgar and Miriam were waking up. He picked them up like they weighed nothing and put them in the van that Lollie drove over. He climbed in back to watch them as we drove to the prison. "How did you get here so quickly?" I asked.

"I couldn't get my head right so I borrowed Drew and we were sitting here talking in your driveway waiting on your call." She said smoking a cigarette and looking out the window. She looked so sad, it broke my heart. "Lollie, what can I do to help you?" I asked worriedly. I loved Lollie like a sister that I never had. She was the sweetest person I had ever met before. "Let me add a few scum to Mr. Rumple's list I found a pedophile sex ring that deals with children being trafficked. Let me track them down and you torture them until I feel better again." She eyed me through her giant glasses. I thought for a moment, nodded and then said, "Deal. Anything you want. I can't stand to see you in so much inner turmoil and pain."

We arrived at the prison and Drew snuck us in carrying the Edgar and Miriam blob I created. I used the key and unlocked the cell to see Jason sobbing on the dirty mattress. Mitch had really done a number to him and that made me happy. I understood how Lollie felt and would do anything I could to help her. "Hello Jason. Here is your food." I said coldly and had Drew dump them on top of Jason. Jason sniffled pathetically and glared at me. "What the fuck are my parents doing here, what did you do?" He snarled at me and pushed them off of him.

"Since they decided to do nothing about you, I gave them their wish of "sticking" together." I said bursting into laughter at my own pun. I stepped out of the cell and was about to lock it back up, plunging Jason into darkness, when Mr. Rumple appeared. "Very nicely done Abby. This is why I enjoy what you do. Jason, this is your punishment." He plunged a needle deep into Jason's neck. "This will make your hunger and all your urges become unrelentless. You will have to eat everyone put in this cell." Mr. Rumple quietly said. I shook my head, I felt trapped. "Drew, you are dismissed. Thank you for helping Abby and Lollie." Mr. Rumple said with his eyes flashing. Drew just nodded like an obedient child and left.

"Lollie I understand you are in a bad place mentally? How would you like to make a deal with me?" Hc said quietly. "No, Lollie don't do it!" I screamed and Mr. Rumple hit me in the head. For a second all I could taste was the floor. "No thank you Mr. Rumple. I respectfully have to decline." She said quietly matching his tone. "Well that's too bad. I think you need some time to get out of that anger. I think spending some personal time with Jason and his parents will do you good."

With that being said he pushed Lolllie into the cell then locked the door. "NOOOOOOOOOO!" I screamed trying to stand back up. "No, you will get her back when you get another one on my list. Adding people to my list is definitely a rule breaker. Since you care so much about her, this is your punishment too. If you want her back out so quickly, better just stick to my list. Understand?" He hissed at me as he grabbed me by my neck.

I nodded and was promptly dropped on the ground. He gave me back the key and left. I tried to open the cell with the key to save her but I didn't have any sort of food to be pushed in so the key didn't work. I was beginning to really hate this arrangement. I wanted to be freed from my contract with Mr. Rumple, but first I had to save Lollie. I drove back to the hospital to see Mortimer. I sobbed on his chest and told him everything that had gone on. He held me and smoothed out my hair with his shaking hand.

"You are going to do what you have to do to save Lollie. When I die, I want to know that you are ok with someone who has your back. Lollie means the world to you just like Aibleen and I do. You need to stop thinking about how you are going to be freed, that is not a luxury we can afford. You have to focus on what Mr. Rumple wants you to do. This is our life now. Welcome to our own personal hell." He whispered as a small line of blood and dribble fell slowly down his chin.

I sighed, I hated it when he was right. I had no choice but to focus on the list of people Mr. Rumple wanted me to take out. I had to rescue Lollie before she was hurt in that cell. I kissed Mortimer deeply then left the hospital keeping my head held up high. I got into the van and lit another cigarette. I unwrapped the list around the key and read the name. I groaned, the next person on my list was my Uncle Charlie. My Uncle Charlie and Jason were best friends. Uncle Charlie was the one that made my mother turn to being a whore. I rewrapped the liste around the key and put the van into drive.

"Hold on Lollie, I am coming as fast as I can." I whispered then stomped on the gas pedal.

Epilogue

Taking care of Uncle Charlie proved to be super easy. All I had to do was log on as T//Error404 on the internet and lure him to me. I stuck a sword I made of ice right into his penis then dragged him to the prison where Drew let me in. I unlocked the cell to see Lollie sitting triumphantly over the dead bodies of Jason and his parents. She smiled and I could see bits of flesh stuck in her teeth. "I have come to rescue you." I whispered to her.

She shook her head no, and hollered for Mr. Rumple. Mr. Rumple appeared curious. "I am ready for that deal Mr. Rumple." Lollie said simply as she used a sharpened piece of bone to pick out the flesh in her teeth. "I am glad to hear that Lollie, what is your deal." He said as he wrapped his arms around her. "I want to be left here in the darkness to consume all the evil brought into here. As a result, I want more people added to your list and I want to be alive as long as Abby is. I will take Mortimer's place." She said snuggling up to Mr. Rumple. He moved a piece of hair out of her face and looked deeply into her eyes. "I have no use for Mortimer, he will remain sick until I am finished with Abby. She is the best I know at being creative. However, I will not keep you in this cell. This cell is designed to hurt the main occupant. I have a special place for you to reside. I will give you everything you want as long as you give into my desires." He kissed her on the forehead. "Lollie you can't do this." I sobbed. I pushed Mr. Rumple off of Lollie and held her close to my chest. "Please don't do this. I need you." I sobbed against her hair. She stood up and hugged me, then walked past me. "You let me continue to help Abby with the list?" She asked.

"Of course, you will have access to the internet and everything you need." Mr. Rumple smiled and closed the cell. He switched out keys from one in his pocket. "This will be your new room." He said softly. He opened the door and I was surprised to find a beautiful bedroom. "Here you will be able to text Abby with locations and names that you can search on the internet. You will be comfortable in the most luxurious room I own. She will bring you the people on the list and you can consume them in any way you see fit. Do we have a deal?" He said in almost a sweet voice.

Lollie walked into the room and smiled. "Deal." She sat on the bed and Mr. Rumple locked the room and gave me the key. "She will not be harmed as long as you are alive, and Mortimer will remain sick as long as you are alive." He left me and all I could do was cradle the key in my hand. Determined, I left the prison. I was going to be the best damn bounty hunter I could be. Eventually, I would find a way to be freed, but until then I might as well do what I know how to do. I smiled and drove to my grandma's house to see Aibleen. It was time to teach my daughter how to take my place if the time ever came. That is a story for another day.

The end

Authors Note

I really hope you enjoy my story. I know that it is farfetched and a little bit out of this world. It is a story I enjoyed writing because it's adding more in depth to my fictional town with Mr. Rumple.

www.ingramcontent.com/pod-product-compliance
Lightning Source LLC
Chambersburg PA
CBHW021200160726
47994CB00001B/296